Sasquatch 4

THE CLONE

Jeffrey B Miley

Table of Contents

Chapter 1

The Find

Ranger Steve Brighton looked up when the front office door opened. Two men dressed in far too much flannel walked in.

Both men looked like they were ready to jump out of their skin. The shorter one was holding a blue terrycloth towel that looked as if it was wrapped around something. The towel looked lightly stained.

Steve asked, "May I help you? What do you have in the towel?"

The taller of the two men answered, "A hand."

Steve jumped up thinking that one of the men was seriously injured. As he rose and headed around his desk, he counted appendages. He stopped. Two men. Four hands. No discernible injury.

Steve asked the most logical question, "Whose hand do you have in the towel?"

The short one answered this time, "We don't know. And it's more like a what, than a who?"

"Lay it down here on the counter," Steve instructed.

As requested, the man holding the towel laid it on the counter.

Steve gently and slowly unfolded the towel.

All three men gasped. What was revealed was indeed a hand. To be clear, it was not a paw. It was two to three times larger than the average male human hand. The back of the hand was covered in fur that traveled up the fingers and around the knuckles.

The fingernails were dirty, ragged and thick. The fingers were short and thick. The palm of the hand, around the pad, was very thick and coarse like sandpaper.

"Where did you find this?"

The tall man introduced himself and his brother, "I'm Scott Milburn and this is my brother, Ted. We're building a hunting cabin on a piece of land that backs up to the lake. It's part of a private farm that has about forty acres of forested area attached."

"You own the farm?" Steve asked.

"No. Long term lease," Scott answered.

"Guys, Raystown Lake is thirty miles long. Where exactly is this farm?" Steve asked.

"Off of 994. Near Trough Creek State Park," Ted offered.

"And how did you come by this huge hand?" the ranger asked.

"We are building a cabin, like we said. We have a portable table saw hooked up to an inverter and several marine batteries that are hooked up to solar panels. When we're done, the solar panels will go on the roof, but for now they top off the batteries that we're using for the saw," Scott explained.

"Okay. The hand, guys. What about the hand?" Brighton pushed.

"I forgot to turn it off and disconnect the saw when we left two days ago. Apparently, whatever this thing is, accidentally turned the saw on and cut its hand off. At least, that's what we figure," Ted explained. "When we came back today, the switch was on, but the saw wasn't running, only because the batteries had run down."

"And the hand was on the table?" the ranger questioned.

"No," Scott answered, "it was lying on the ground all covered with ants. We washed it off and then wrapped it up in this towel. We didn't know where else to take it."

"Have you told anyone else?" Steve wanted to know.

"Not a soul," Ted answered.

"Keep it that way. Please. I need to get Penn State's Wildlife and Fisheries Lab to look at this. They'll know what it is," Brighton explained.

"We kind of thought it was a sasquatch. Don't you think?" Scott asked.

"That determination is above my pay grade. It could be some kind of anomaly like a freakishly large racoon hand that swelled for some reason. I've seen the most unbelievable explanations for natural abnormalities. Give me your numbers, and I'll call you when I know something."

The men gladly left their cellphone numbers. They both thanked the ranger and left.

As they walked to the truck, Scott said to Ted, "That ain't no bloated racoon hand. I think we should take our rifles to the cabin when we go back this weekend. Something big is roaming those forests, and it's probably pissed about losing its hand on our saw."

"I hear you, Scottie. That poor ranger is gonna be in for a surprise."

"No, bro. He already knows it's a sasquatch. He just can't say so. Above his pay grade? What a joke. That was Ranger Steve Brighton. He's the Senior Resident Ranger for the Southwestern Pennsylvania Region."

"How do you know that?" Ted asked, astonished that Scott would know that.

"It was on that plaque on the wall by the front door. He's the top dog in the region. Nothing is above his pay grade."

They got in their pickup and left.

Angela Summers answered her phone. She saw who it was on caller ID--Steve Brighton, the cute ranger over at Raystown. She hoped the call was personal.

It wasn't. Angela, who ran the Penn State Wildlife and Fisheries Lab on campus, would be disappointed.

"Angie, I've got a weird one here. Two outdoorsmen just dropped off a disembodied hand."

"What? A human hand?"

"No. I never used the word human. This has to be our favorite nonexistent hominid," he teased.

"Wait. You mean Bigfoot?"

He laughed, "Haven't you seen the insurance commercials? His name is Daryl."

"Are you serious about this?" she asked.

"Angie, I've never seen such compelling evidence. Can I drive it over and get it in your line up?"

"Sure, Steve. But I require flowers and a box of chocolates before you get in the queue."

He rolled his eyes. This woman, attractive as she was, was always hitting on him when he called. He played along, but there was something about her that reeked of desperation. Besides, he had Cindy and she was a handful on her own. He didn't need complications.

He wanted her cooperation so, once again, he played along, "How about a bag of Skittles?"

"Well, if that's the best you can do. Aren't you the lead ranger in the region? You'd think you would want to put your best foot forward and woo a girl," Angie giggled.

This whole bit was growing tiresome. He sighed.

"Skittles or nothing," he stated.

"Bring it in, ranger." It was her turn to sigh, "I'll put you at the front of the line. But I want M&M's, not Skittles."

"You got it. I'll be there in an hour or so."

She was glad the call was over. It was obvious the man would never be interested. She didn't know why she treated him so well.

Maybe she could get him back for being such an elusive jerk. She grabbed the receiver of the phone on her desk and put it to her ear as she dialed a number.

When she was finished, she hung up and smiled. The person she had just called upon was over the top interested.

Angie would sometimes call certain persons or agencies that would have interest in items that were being tested in the lab.

In return, she would see some monetary compensation. Not much, but enough to take two or three cruises a year. No one ever got hurt by the arrangement.

Not ever.

Chapter 2

The Rangers

Ranger Tom Bollman walked slowly towards the man who was fishing from the bank of the lake. He was a rough looking character.

He had a bald head, goatee, multiple earrings in both ears and tattoos that covered both arms and halfway up his neck. Tom had seen the man's motorcycle parked on the shoulder of the road.

"Good morning, sir. How are they biting?" Ranger Bollman asked nicely.

"Fuck off and leave me alone! I'm just fishing. I ain't bothering nobody," the fisherman said gruffly.

"Do you possess a fishing license?"

"I told you to get lost. Now take off before it's too late."

"I have to insist that you show me your license, or I must write you a summons."

"I don't have a license. So what are you going to do about it? Piss off before I have to hurt you!" the offensive man warned.

Tom was unflappable, "May I see your driver's license, please."

"That's it, asshole!" the man said and walked straight at Tom. The fisherman threw a punch. Tom stepped to the left and countered with a right uppercut.

The man stumbled backwards. He outweighed Tom by at least fifty pounds. What he didn't know was that Tom, now age thirty-six, had been a ranked Golden Gloves fighter in his twenties.

He went after Tom again. The resultant action ended with the bigger man landing on his ass. He shook his head to clear the fog and looked up at Tom.

"You're pretty good with your fists, Mister Boy Scout, but how are you against a knife?"

With a switchblade in hand, the man lunged at Tom.

Tom sidestepped the man and punched him sharply in the kidneys. The man let out an 'oof' sound and went down.

The man sat up and looked up into Tom's face. "You win. Arrest me already."

"Nope. Just want your driver's license."

The man reached into his back pocket for his wallet. He flipped through his IDs and credit cards and came up with his license and handed it to Tom.

Tom pulled his ticketing book from his back pocket and wrote out the violation which had an associated $250 fine.

"Here's your ticket. You know, I probably would have let you off with a warning. Now collect your pole, get on your bike and leave. If I catch you again, I will take you in and let the Justice of the Peace increase the fine."

"Okay, buddy. Just give me a minute to get my pole and I'm out of here."

Tom watched as the man walked up the hill to the road. He mounted his cycle and jumped on the starter and the cycle roared to life. He then gave Tom a one finger salute and drove off.

Bollman then went back to his own car and headed to the Ranger District Office. On the way there, he thought about all the tough guys he had run into over the years. When someone pushed back against them, they usually gave in. Bullies are never in a fight for the long haul if they don't have a clear advantage.

Once he arrived at the office, he related his experience to his boss.

Steve just stared at him for a second and then said, "A guy pulls a knife on you, and you don't arrest him? Why not?"

"He wasn't going to stab me. At most he was going to slice me and hope that that would be enough to scare me off. I've seen his type before. A real killer he was not. There's a reason why he's in love with the tough guy look: the piercings, tattoos and motorcycle," Bollman explained.

Steve had to ask, "And what reason is that?"

"He likes the trashy women who like the bad boy routine. They're easy and adventurous. And some like it rough. All that window dressing is bait for the bad girl that likes to get beat up and dominated."

"And how do you know all this, Doctor Freud?"

"Exactly, I was a Human Behavioral Studies major in college. I got my master's in Psychology. You knew that," Ranger Bollman pointed out.

"Yeah. I know. But sometimes I forget how smart you are and that you are slumming working here with us. And why are you doing this work, instead of counseling or something that makes the big bucks?" Steve asked, probably for the dozenth time over the six years that they had worked together.

"Come on boss. You know the answer. All my studies led me to the conclusion that all people are assholes and are beyond help. Present company excluded, of course. And besides, I like the great outdoors."

And probably for the dozenth time, Steve laughed at the answer. He always stated that all people are assholes, except Steve, of course.

Ranger Milt Cox was on patrol around the Seven Points Marina. He loved being a ranger. He enjoyed the water and the wildlife that inhabited this part of Pennsylvania.

Milt was a deer hunter and couldn't wait for deer season to begin in a month. He also hated deer season because too many hunters thought that the rules didn't apply to them. They habitually blurred the lines between buck and doe season. And too many exceeded their legal limit.

Those same miscreants used firearms during bow season and regular rifles during muzzle loader and flintlock season. The season for his own hunting always seemed to be marred by finding the rule breakers while he was going after his own deer.

And he would never forget that the only two times he had ever been shot was while apprehending deer hunters.

The first time was an accident. A man's rifle was falling out of the bed of his pickup, and the man tried to catch it. It discharged, hitting Milt in the shoulder.

His wife almost died from worry. She was convinced he was going to die from an infection or blood poisoning. She had gotten those notions from her gossipy friend, Tammy. Tammy was one of those people who always knew someone whom had experienced unusual tragedy.

Milt couldn't stand the woman, But Charlene, Milt's wife, loved the woman. She was her best friend.

The second time, he was shot was by an irate hunter who didn't believe he was a real ranger. The man shot him in the leg. Milt, in self-defense, shot and killed the man.

The worse part for Milt was the guilt over not feeling guilty. Now there's one less jackass in the world, was his take. But he knew that taking a human life should have affected him more deeply, at least that is what everyone told him.

Milt really was a decent man, with good values, whom did not suffer fools gladly. It was something with which he and Tom Bollman were in agreement. The percentage of assholes in the world was on the rise and many of them found their way into the woods.

Milt also liked patrolling around the marina. He was saving up for a boat. Charlene wasn't exactly on board with the idea. Tammy had filled her with statistics about boating accidents and drownings in recreational areas. Another reason for him not to like the woman.

He had seen a Yamaha AR240 for only $48,000. He already had $21,000 saved. His preference would be to pay cash. He had a great distrust of banks and hated credit cards.

He and Charlene lived in his mom's house. It was the home he grew up in, and he had inherited it when his mother passed, over eleven years ago.

He had no mortgage, which made him happy. He and Charlene both drove nice used cars that were bought and paid for.

They had no children after thirteen years of marriage. He was glad. Their money was their own. Charlene allowed him to save for his dream boat, as long as they went on a cruise every two years. They already had been on six.

For Milt, it had been a quiet day.

Ranger Tom Deering wished his day were going differently. He had already rousted two vagrants out of a drainage pipe near the dam.

He was now headed to Gladys Bomberger's house. She was a little old lady who lived on the very edge of the state game lands.

She called once a month with a complaint or a Bigfoot sighting. Anything to have someone to talk to her.

Tom didn't dislike the old woman, but she was what he called an SLTW, sneaky little time waster.

Why Steve made them entertain this behavior was beyond Tom. Maybe this time she would have some homemade cookies. Usually when she called, it would coincide with her having just baked something delicious. That was the up side of handling her made up complaints.

He pulled onto her gravel drive, which was over fifty yards long. He parked out front by her washline and little vegetable garden that she tended.

She was standing on the front porch, waving.

He got out of his car thinking, *please let her have baked chocolate chip cookies today.* That was for what he currently had a craving.

"Oh, Thomas, I'm so glad they sent you. I just baked a batch of my chocolate chip cookies that you like so much."

All he could think was, *yes, there is a God.*

"Oh, Thomas. You won't believe what I saw."

"Hi, Gladys. Why don't you let me sample some of those fantastic chocolate chip cookies with a glass of milk? And you can tell me all about what you saw."

They went to her kitchen, and he took a seat at the table. This was how the routine always went.

She set a plate, with eight beautiful, golden brown cookies as his own mom called them, in front of him. She also set a tall glass of ice cold 2% milk in front of him as well. The little boy inside of him was jumping for joy.

"So, Gladys, what did you see today?" he asked politely as he lifted the first cookie to his mouth.

Oh, Thomas," she started, as she always did, "a Bigfoot monster walked through my back yard this morning. But the poor thing only had one hand."

This is new, he thought to himself. *She never has any outstanding details to give.*

"Was it still eight feet tall, with long stringy hair all over?" he remembered from previous descriptions.

"Yes, but the poor thing's fur was matted with blood in places," she told him.

He set cookie number three back down on the plate.

"Gladys, why would you say such a thing? Bloody fur? Really?"

"Oh, I knew you wouldn't believe me, so I got my Polaroid OneStep out of the closet. I bought film for it not that long ago. I got it as a Christmas gift from my daughter-in-law, Carol. Never liked her much, but this was a nice gift. Of course, that was the Christmas of 2006. But the camera still works."

"Gladys, are you telling me you took a picture of the creature?" Tom asked incredulously.

"Yessiree. Right here it is, dear. Are you enjoying your cookies?"

Tom answered, "Best cookies ever," as he grabbed for the Polaroid. He looked closely at the photo. Then he sat in stunned silence.

This was a damn Polaroid. She couldn't fake it.

The beast was standing next to the old potting shed in her back yard. Tom got up and looked out the back window at the potting shed.

"How tall would you say that potting shed is, Gladys?"

"Well, you step up about six inches and when Mr. Bomberger was still alive, he could just stand up straight in it at the peak. He was six foot, so I guess it has to be about seven feet tall. Why dear?"

"The animal in the photo is a good foot taller than the shed," Tom said almost in a daze.

"Well, I've always told you he was about eight feet tall, haven't I?" she asked sweetly.

"May I please keep this photo? I need to show it to my boss."

"Yes, dear. And let me get a bag for the rest of your cookies. Unless you want to stay and finish them."

He knew that she needed the company, and the photo wasn't going anywhere, and this is where the cold milk was. All good reasons to stay.

"I'll stay for a while, thank you. So what did the creature do after you took the photo?" he asked.

"He just looked at me with his pained eyes. The poor thing really didn't look as healthy as he usually does. You know, the blood and all. And look," she said, pointing to the photo, "You can tell the one hand is missing, right there."

He looked closely. The right hand was lighter where the palm was exposed. But where the left hand should have been, there was nothing.

He stared at the photo as she continued, "Eventually, he just walked away. The amazing thing is that when he comes to visit, I'm never scared. He just takes a shortcut through my yard, and every now and then he takes some of my vegetables. I don't mind. We all have to eat, don't we?"

"Have you ever left him some cookies or pie?" Tom asked, half joking, half serious.

"No, dear. Apparently, they only attract rangers."

Chapter 3

The Sasquatch

After it lost its hand, it ran through the forest in misery. Never had the beast felt pain the way he was feeling it now.

He moved deeper into the woods where he knew no other creatures would bother him. The creatures that he feared most, and was most curious about, were the mostly hairless ones. They were so strange in their looks and habits.

They were dangerous. In his many years of roaming the woods, he had been shot at seven times. One time he was hit. It was extremely bothersome and took almost three months to heal. He almost died because of his limited ability to hunt and feed himself.

Now this. Was it a trap? He was just being his usual curious self. The hairless were setting up what he thought was a shelter. They put together a lot of things. They lived in some of the things they built, and they sat in other things that moved and took them places. Movers was how he perceived cars and trucks.

He stayed away from the hairless. He was extremely shy and reclusive. And too curious for his own good.

His kind lived to be well over one hundred. They lived out of sight from the humans that populated the world.

He was seventy-three years old and basically middle-aged. Men had tried to catch him, kill him and expose his existence his entire life. He thought of those humans as the hairless. He didn't hate them, he just feared them and found them odd.

He was in his mid-twenties when the town of Aitch was flooded over to create Raystown Lake. This was the region that had the most potential for a hydro-electric dam and a flood control zone. The Army Corps of Engineers did the honors.

The creature's home was in the valley near the town. The rising water drove him out. He had seen a flash flood or two, but this was different. The water never receded and his home was lost.

The sasquatches were a dying breed. Their habitat was being encroached upon at an alarming rate and diseases brought here by the hairless humans had decimated the population.

The last time he had mated was over three years ago, with a female in Centre County. He had no idea whether he had any progeny or not. He wasn't even sure that his mate was still alive.

The species preferred solitude and spent most of their time engaged in basic survival. This particular sasquatch was capable of using crude tools and has exhibited limited cognitive thinking.

Rock throwing was his best skill. Using stones to cut, smash and scrape were within his skill set as well. He was also capable of using sharpened sticks to kill prey in their burrows or warrens.

Sasquatches were omnivorous and ate meat, fruits, vegetable and carrion. They were actually hunters, gatherers and opportunists.

And the highways of Pennsylvania, which are known for dead deer littering their roadside, would be worse off if it weren't for sasquatches grabbing the easy meal when no one was looking.

In fact, many of the deer killed on those roadways were driven out of relative safety by ingenious sasquatches, using passing cars and trucks as a way of killing their next meal.

The pain continued to wash over the handless sasquatch in waves. He wished that there was another creature with whom he could share his pain. He thought of Gladys, although he had no clue as to what she was called. Her eyes were always kind, and she showed no fear.

He did a walk by. He stood by the small shelter at the back of the house. She came out and pointed something at him. A moment of fear passed through him, but nothing bad happened. He couldn't bring himself to stay.

He walked away in pain and was almost sad about what might have been.

He watched her place as a hairless mover came and an armed hairless got out. He had seen this kind before with some kind of weapon on his hip. They had authority over the others.

His mind wandered for a second as he marveled at how fast the movers were and that sometimes they held more than just one of the hairless. This mover had lights on top. That meant something about the hairless one's authority as well.

He saw the old hairless female greet the one with authority in a very friendly way. They entered the dwelling. A short time later, the one in authority left.

His arm hurt badly. The sasquatch heard whimpering and then realized it was himself. The beast needed help.

He began walking back to the old woman's house. When he got to the back yard, he stood silently, waiting. The creature had seen her many times before through the invisible portions of the walls.

It wasn't long before the old woman came to one of the windows that looked out into the back yard. Before long, she was on the rear patio stoop.

Gladys couldn't believe what she was seeing. The ranger had been gone only about fifteen minutes, and there stood the eight-foot-tall man ape in the middle of her back yard. He looked like he wanted something. He looked needy.

She was struck with a short bout of bad judgment and a long streak of compassion. Walking out the back door ,she began to approach the sasquatch.

The old woman stood six feet away. The pitiful beast held out his handless arm for her to see.

"Oh, sweetie. Where's your hand? That must hurt something fierce," she said as she reached out.

The sasquatch quickly pulled his hand back into his chest.

"Honey, you stay right there. I have something that might help." She walked to her garage, where inside she had a huge chest freezer. Gladys had two ten-pound bags of ice left over from a little party she held at Christmas last year. They sat in the freezer, unused all this time.

She grabbed her two-and-a-half-gallon bucket. Next, she poured the ice from one bag into the container. Adding a little water, she began to stir.

Gladys then hauled the bucket back to the big beast, who was still standing in her yard.

She pointed to her arm and plunged it into the bucket. Next she pointed to the creature's arm and nodded, "Go ahead. Don't be a baby."

The sasquatch stepped forward and did as she showed him. At first it screeched loudly, but kept its stub in the water.

Five minutes passed, and the sasquatch began to relax. His whimpering had stopped altogether. Gladys had helped him relieve his pain, and she had made a new friend.

There would be no more phone calls to the rangers about the sasquatch.

Her sasquatch.

The beast felt sweet relief. The ice was numbing the pain. This hairless female was now his ally. In all the world, he finally found a friend.

He knew that he saw kindness in her eyes. He, in his own primitive way, was grateful to whatever controlled the universe.

A creature to share life with. It was something that he had always wanted. Daryl had tried to befriend his mating partner years ago, but there was no interest on her part.

He now had a friend.

Chapter 4

Wheels Start Turning

Tom showed Steve the Polaroid the next day when he came into work. He had spent quite a bit of time looking it over the night before. It was nothing short of amazing.

Steve held it, while standing beside his desk, under fluorescent lighting. Then he took it over by the window to see if natural light changed things.

Tom waited patiently for Steve to say something. He didn't.

The Senior Resident Ranger sat back down at his desk and tilted his desk light. He pulled out a strong magnifying loop that he had for looking at insects more closely.

"You know, this might be the most convincing and authentic photo of a sasquatch that I have ever seen. I have something to tell you, since we are on the subject of sasquatch," Steve said.

"Before you do, I have something extra to tell you about something Gladys said that may have you looking at the photo again," Tom interrupted.

"Go ahead, Tom. I'm all ears."

"Gladys said the thing was covered in blood. It's hard to tell in the Polaroid. She also said it was missing a hand."

"Which one?" Steve asked, already knowing the answer.

"Look again at the photo. The left appears to be missing," Tom instructed. "Or should I say, the left doesn't appear at all?"

Steve looked again. He shook his head yes.

"Now my turn, Tom. Two men dropped in yesterday. They had found something at the site of a cabin they are building. It seems they had set up a table saw and forgot to turn it off. They found a severed hand. By the size and condition, it was most definitely not human. I think we now have a picture of its owner."

"What do we do?" Tom asked.

"I already did something. I drove over to State College and dropped the hand off for analysis at the Wildlife and Fisheries Lab," Steve told him.

"Oh, crap! Did Angie attack you again?"

"No. I kept her at bay with a bag of M&M's. She's a piece of work, though. She said they should know something in forty-eight hours."

"Okay. I'll hit the road and go on patrol," Tom announced.

Steve began preparation for a trip to support thirteen small state parks near Pittsburgh. All were under his jurisdiction.

He would be gone for two weeks starting next Monday. This, being Wednesday, assured him of hearing what the lab had to say about the hand before he left.

He worked well into the early evening.

Gladys had coaxed the sasquatch to down an entire bottle of aspirin. She wasn't sure if it would work to alleviate his discomfort or possibly cause him great stomach upset.

Her kind soul could not sit by while he suffered. The ice and aspirin must have helped somewhat, for the giant creature laid down in her back yard and fell asleep.

And he snored terribly.

Gladys listened to him for over an hour, while rocking on her back porch. She couldn't believe how something so large could be so gentle.

She had never even owned a dog or a cat since childhood. Mr. Bomberger was highly allergic to animal dander. It was odd that plants and pollen never bothered him. Only animals.

Now she had a pet sasquatch. She too had seen the insurance commercials that had populated every channel the last few months. That woman spokesperson was talking to a sasquatch and called him Bigfoot. He took offense and said his name was Daryl.

Seemed as good a name as any. The sasquatch now had a name. She would teach him his new name tomorrow.

As she rocked, she brainstormed about what else she might have in her arsenal to relieve his pain. Her biggest fear was infection.

Her second biggest concern was that Daryl may not be able to hunt and gather his food the way he could when he was healthy. Tomorrow she would order a side of beef from McKinney's Butcher Shop.

She saw that she had plenty of room in her freezer when she had retrieved the ice for Daryl. She would make sure he had plenty to eat. It was the least she could do for the poor thing.

She remembered something and headed into the house. Mr. Bomberger had tried many different things to fight the open sores that he suffered from his long bout with diabetes. Two things that he used as natural antibiotics were oregano oil and ginger based products. She still had both.

Tomorrow she would administer both to Daryl, in the hopes it would help him from getting an infection. His wound was a serious one.

That night she prayed that sasquatches had strong immune systems. She wanted her new friend around for a long time.

Angie sat in the parking garage for almost an hour. She was pissed to high heaven, as her dad used to say. Her contact was late, and she was thinking about leaving.

In her back seat was a cryogenic transport container. It was an expensive piece of equipment used to transport tissue that was at risk of decaying and deteriorating quickly.

The hand had already been unprotected for over twenty-four hours before it got into her hands. Her customer wanted the deterioration stopped immediately, which explained the need for the cryo unit.

She wasn't sure who the end customer actually was. Angie knew the man she dealt with was a go between for several sketchy individuals and organizations. She really didn't want to know who they were. All she wanted was her money.

Finally, a BMW pulled into the spot next to hers. It was the man she had come to know as Julian. No more, no less. Just Julian.

He got out of his car and opened up her passenger door and got in.

"Do you have the package?"

"Yes. Did you bring a container which to transfer it?"

"No. No one said anything about that."

"Well, that box is a fricking $15,000 cryogenics container. I need to get it back to the lab tonight, so it's not going with you. That's for damn sure!" she informed him.

"Angie, I don't have a container to put the package inside. Let me take it, and I'll make sure you get it back."

"No way, Julian! They'll charge me with theft, and they'll want to know where it went. You wouldn't want that, would you?" she asked, thinking that she was negotiating with this man on an even playing field.

She wasn't.

He pulled a pistol with a silencer and shot her point blank in the middle of the forehead.

She coughed and gagged for a moment. Her eyes fluttered, and then she slumped backwards against the driver's side window.

Julian hopped up out of the passenger seat and closed the door. He then opened the back door. He retrieved the cryo unit and transferred it to his own back seat.

He got back into the BMW, started it up, reversed it out of the space and drove away.

Angela Summers, Director of the Penn State Wildlife and Fisheries Lab, was dead. She would be found by a security guard making her rounds, two hours later.

In less than two hours, before Angela had been discovered, Julian had delivered the prize to his customer in a small barn on the outskirts of State College.

"So tell me again, why you had to kill the girl?"

"She wouldn't let me have the cryogenic unit. I didn't want your merchandise to spoil, General. So I shot her," Julian explained.

"My God, Julian! You could have gone to the mini-market, gotten a bag of ice and a cardboard box from their dumpster. It would have kept just fine until you met me here. And now I need a new contact on the inside of the lab, because of you," the General enlightened him. "We also have to worry about whether the parking garage uses still photos or video cameras or both. You are now a serious liability to us. And that poor, pretty girl didn't have to die," the older man said as he nodded to one his men.

For the second time that night, a pistol with a silencer was employed. Two shots to the heart and Julian crumbled like a sack of potatoes.

The General asked the shooter, "You know what to do?"

"Yessir. The BMW gets chopped and sold. The money will go to the young woman's family, anonymously. Julian will be fed to our hungrier experiments."

"Good man," the General said with a smile. "Now, grab that box and give me a hand."

One of the General's men picked up the box and handed it to him.

"Really? No one is going to laugh? Grab the box and give me a hand is hilarious. There's a hand in the box. Get it?"

The three men with him all began laughing.

He held up a hand, "Nope. Too late. You had your chance to get the joke. If I have to explain it, then it's ruined."

He carried the box to his waiting government limo. He got into the backseat. The long, black car pulled out of the barn, heading to the main building on the government compound which was almost ten miles away.

Chapter 5

Missing

On Thursday morning, Steve called the Penn State Wildlife and Fisheries Lab. A young woman whom he had spoken to on several other occasions answered. Her name was Tina.

"Hi, Tina. This is Ranger Steve Brighton, over in Huntingdon. I expected Angie to answer this number. Is she in?"

The young woman burst into tears. She was trying to talk while sobbing. Steve couldn't understand a word that she uttered.

"Tina, honey, calm down. I can't understand a thing you're saying."

Before she could start up again, a stern male voice came on the line, "Who is this?"

Steve was taken aback by the brusque tone, "This is Ranger Steven Brighton, Raystown Lake Rangers Station. What is wrong with Tina?"

"She's upset. We all are. What did you say to her?"

"I asked to speak to Angela. She should be expecting my call. To whom am I speaking?"

"This is Phil Reynard. Angela's second in charge. I'm afraid, Ranger Brighton, that I have bad news."

Steve didn't like the way this conversation was going at all. "Phil, just tell me what's wrong."

"Angie was shot dead last night in a parking garage near the campus."

Steve couldn't talk. He was shocked by the news. He then immediately felt bad because his mind turned towards the safety of the hand he had dropped off. He wasn't sure how to ask about it. What was the protocol there after a coworker was murdered?

Phil let him off the hook, "How may I help you? I assume you're calling about business."

"Yes, Phil. I am so sorry for your loss. Truly. I did have a question about a very important sample I dropped off on Tuesday. Could you check on it for me?"

"Yes, of course, Steve. What was the nature of the sample?"

Steve tried to sound as official and intelligent as he could, "Phil, I dropped off what is believed to be a hominid hand."

"A human hand," he asked, startled by what the sample was. "Shouldn't that have gone to the Medical Examiner?"

"I didn't say human hand. It was a hand. We are pretty sure it belonged to a hominid, but human it was not," Steve explained.

"Bigfoot?" Phil questioned.

"That's what we were thinking," Ranger Brighton confirmed.

"Okay. Let me check. I can't wait to see that myself."

Steve waited on hold and listened to tinny elevator music, at least that was how he always described badly recorded instrumentals.

After about the sixth song, he wondered if he was somehow cut off. But he reasoned that if he were still hearing the music, that couldn't be the case. Maybe Phil had to calm another hysterical employee that was having problems dealing with Angie's demise.

He even took to mulling that over for a while. Shot dead in a parking garage. That certainly doesn't happen to regular people very often. Was Angie leading a double life? Selling drugs? She did go on a lot of cruises every year, he thought to himself while waiting. He shook off that idea. She wasn't the type to sell drugs.

He was about to hang up when Phil came back on the line, "Ranger Brighton, Angie didn't enter any samples on Tuesday or Wednesday. And before you ask, she didn't have anyone else do it either. The only thing unusual is that she signed out a cryogenic transport unit. It's a very expensive piece of equipment, and it is missing. She did that on Tuesday afternoon. Your sample is not here."

Steve was silent, trying to think about what this meant.

"Ranger Brighton, are you still there?"

"Yes, Phil. I'm here. Are you sure that you've checked all possibilities? Could she have handed it off to someone special? And what is a cryogenic transport unit used for?"

"She wouldn't have given it to anyone outside the lab. A cryogenic transport unit is used to preserve live tissue while it travels from one place to another."

"Just asking, Phil. Would it make sense that she would use this cryogenic transport unit to move a severed hand from one place to another if she wanted to keep the hand from decomposing?"

"Yes. But why would she do that?"

"I don't know, Phil. Why are two things missing at the same time? My sample and your transport unit."

"Ranger, I don't like what you are saying. And remember, your sample is not officially missing because it was never officially here. Are you done with me?" Phil asked.

"Yes, Phil. Thank you. And once again, I'm sorry for your loss."

As Steve hung up, he said aloud to an empty office, "I'm even more sorry for my loss." And then a pang of guilt washed over him because of his insensitivity.

In a secluded government lab, in the Rothrock State Forest, a group of scientists formulated a plan for their new sample.

The lead scientist on the project was Doctor Gustav Nolten. He was respected in the field of genetic engineering, as well as his two respected colleagues, Doctors Jonathan Dougherty and Wilmer Ganse.

The first task at hand was to verify the species from the hand tissue. That was done rather swiftly. It was hominid, just as suspected. In fact, more hominin than expected.

The next order of business was verifying the genetic makeup of the creature. It was discovered that the specimen had twenty-four chromosome pairs compared to a human's twenty-three.

The creature was believed to be a form of man from more than fifty thousand years in the past. It was primitive, yet possessing a fairly large brain cavity. This was not the first specimen of this type that they had studied over the years.

The tissues from the specimen showed that the beast enjoyed good health and strange, if not accelerated, restorative properties. In simpler terms, it possessed the ability to heal quickly.

The restorative properties did not lead to a conclusion of regenerative properties. It would not regrow the hand or any other part of its anatomy.

It took two weeks to complete all the tests on the specimen. It was now time for the cloning to begin. That was what was so different about this experiment.

It was time to stop cloning and modifying the well-known species in the forest. It was time to deal with this relatively unknown family of creatures.

Two weeks after the call with Phil, Steve was returning from his tour of the Pittsburgh area state parks. All was in order and operating quite well.

The thirteen parks were covered by only eight rangers. They were small parks and several were patrolled by the

Pennsylvania State Police as well. Not much happened there, except for the occasional drug bust and fishermen without their licenses.

Their size and locations made them less than ideal for hunting, but nearby creeks provided some excellent fishing opportunities.

During the year, most of Steve's time was taken up by Rothrock and Moshannon State Forests. He had five rangers in each forest. When he needed additional men, he sent his Raystown guys to augment wherever they were needed.

He also had over three dozen Fish and Game officers that he could call upon when needed. He was blessed with a good crew.

He was glad to be back home. His girlfriend, Cindy, had cared for his pup. He had a Golden Retriever puppy named T-Rex. He was four months old and full of mischief. He loved Cindy and the dog.

He wasn't sure who he missed the most. If he ever decided, he would keep it to himself.

Cindy worked for a data collection agency. They designed polls and studies on everything. She was known as a Class A Data Collection Miner. She was at the top of her game.

She had a knack for finding information that others found impossible to come by. He gave her a little assignment before he left. He wanted her to find out as much as she could about Angela Summers and the lab in general.

Once he was relaxed, the dog walked, the supper dishes washed and put away, he inquired as to her success.

Cindy was a very attractive redhead with bright green, almond shaped eyes. She was petite but very athletic looking. She wished for longer legs, but since that wasn't happening, she wore heels quite often. Steve liked that.

He wasn't a GQ poster boy, but at six one and two hundred and thirty pounds, he presented very nicely. He had brown hair, brown eyes and dimples that Cindy loved to poke. He found that sometimes a bit annoying.

They were a solid couple and complimented one another intellectually. Spiritually was a different story. She was a dyed in the wool Methodist, and he was running from a childhood spent in the Catholic school system. He stilled prayed but no church attendance. They made their relationship work.

She couldn't wait to share what she had found concerning his request. Cindy had put in a lot of work just to please him.

"Your Angie is very interesting. She has worked at the lab for eight years. She was recruited to be the director. It wasn't an extremely lucrative position, but it was prestigious. With overtime pay, some of her lab technicians made more money than her.

"Anyway, after year two, extra money began filtering into her bank accounts. And she began the habit of taking two or three Caribbean cruises a year. Mysterious, huh?"

"Wait. You were able to access her bank accounts and see large deposits?" Steve asked.

"Yes, I was able to access her accounts. Don't ask how. And no, there weren't any huge deposits," she replied.

"About five times a year she would make unusual deposits of between $1,500 to $3,000. Not exactly high roller type of money, but I couldn't find a reasonable explanation as to how she acquired this money.

"Over a period of almost six years, she had deposited an additional $68,000 above and beyond her salary. That seems significant."

"Well, she was pretty. Maybe she had a sugar daddy that she kept satisfied. Or she could have been an occasional high-priced call girl." he suggested.

"Really? Why do men immediately tie every outcome to sex?"

"Because, according to TV, that is usually the common denominator for everything," he explained.

"You need to watch more wholesome shows. Now may I go on?"

He smiled. She was adorable when she was mad, "Go ahead. I'm all ears."

"No, you need a haircut rather badly. Once we get you trimmed up, you'll be all ears with them big flappers of yours," she teased.

"Just continue," he said, pretending to be angry himself.

Let me just say that if you filed a complaint about your missing sample, you wouldn't be the first. And if you filed a complaint about your test results being leaked, you wouldn't be the first. You getting my drift?"

"So she sold samples and leaked reports as a part-time job? Something else you want to tell me?"

"Did you know that the federal government has a top-secret facility in Rothrock State Forest?"

"It's my State Park, honey. There isn't much I don't know," he said, a little irked that she thought he wouldn't know.

"Okay. What exactly do they do there…honey?"

She was making a point.

"I don't know, Cindy. I believe the words 'top secret' are used for a reason. So, no, I do not know what they do there."

"Nobody does, Steve. Nobody," she emphasized.

"Top secret," he countered. "It's working. Why are you even bringing that place up? We were talking about Angie."

"There's a rumor that it is a genetics lab," she said.

"You lost me at rumor."

"Who would want a sasquatch hand? Think. A severed sasquatch hand," she said, dramatically.

"Maybe somebody thought it was like that story, 'The Monkey's Paw.' They think they're getting three wishes," he joked.

"Steve, she didn't enter your sasquatch hand into the lab line up. She signs out a cryogenic transport thingy, and then she gets whacked in a parking garage at night and now the cryo thingy is missing," she concluded.

"Whacked?" he laughed.

"Yes, a bullet smack dab in the middle of her forehead. That's not robbery. That's an assassination by a pro!"

He didn't know the details of the shooting. He assumed some punk kid tried robbing her, and she got shot. But a bullet to the forehead doesn't suggest a shot of desperation. As Cindy said, it sounded like a pro shot her.

"Okay. Let's say it was a purposeful kill. Why do you assume a connection with the government lab?" he asked.

"I was saving this for last," Cindy said. She went to the sideboard and picked up a scrapbook.

"Bear in mind that the secret facility was opened in 1973. The same year that all eyes were on Raystown, the Army Corps of Engineers and the hydroelectric dam," she instructed as she handed the scrapbook to him.

For the next hour, he read article after article that she had copied and pasted into the book. When he was done, all he could say was, "Wow!"

"And lastly, I asked myself why they looked outside of their own ranks for a director?" she posed.

"Who?"

"The lab, honey! The lab! Penn State is famous for being a closed system. Promote from within, rise through the ranks. You know. That kind of mindset. Well, they didn't do that with Angela. She was an outsider from North Carolina."

"And?"

"The previous director, Maxine Peterman, was hired in 1970. She had a Doctorate in Biological Sciences. Angela had a Masters in Biology. She was a step down.

And Maxine also had a history of money showing up unexplained," she informed him.

"Whoa. Now you're scaring me. You can't tell me you looked up bank records from when before computers were used," he told her.

"No. Even I couldn't do that. But you told me this was super important to you, so I pulled out all the stops. I found two older women who are living in retirement homes in the State College area. They both worked for Maxine."

"You went and interviewed them?"

"Yep. And it was illuminating."

"Cindy, I didn't expect you to go this far. But since you did, what did you find out?"

"Maxine had her masters and was the director of the lab, and she still wasn't making squat. Women's pay was severely depressed. That was the seventies for you," she exclaimed. "Anyway, in the mid-seventies, military officers began visiting the lab. No one knew why. Maxine hosted them when they showed up. Then things started to change."

Steve was on the edge of his seat. He hated to admit that she had him hooked, especially after the scrapbook.

"Change how?"

"Maxine became a fashion plate, wearing expensive clothing, jewelry and shoes. And then the vacations began. She and her husband started taking annual trips to Europe.

The ladies said that Maxine told them that she had inherited some money, but there was never any real explanation.

"Even the ladies I interviewed made the connection between the military showing up and her windfall, especially in light of missing samples and leaked reports.

"Just like with Angela. The pattern began in the mid-seventies, same time as the secret base being established. And with all those weird articles….well, you have to see what I see. Right?"

"Yes. I see it. I am a hairsbreadth away from believing all of it. But none of it is provable, and none of it gets my sasquatch hand back."

There was a moment of silence before Steve spoke again, "I'm curious. You found these old ladies who worked with Maxine. What about Maxine herself. Is she still alive?"

Cindy smiled a broad smile, "Thank you. I almost forgot, and this is interesting. Maxine retired right before Angie was recruited. The poor woman didn't last two weeks. She was killed in an auto accident. She lost control of her car one night while driving to the supermarket.

"I was able to hack the police report. The investigating officer found it strange for several reasons. The husband said she got a phone call earlier in the evening. That wasn't that unusual, but she made an excuse that she was out of some ingredients for a recipe she wanted to make the next day.

"So, question one that the investigator had: Why couldn't she wait until the next day to get the grocery item? She was killed on a stretch of road traveling away from all of the local supermarkets and in the opposite direction of her home. That gave rise to the second question: Where was she really headed? So what do you think?"

"Someone was tying up loose ends. Old dead women can't talk. Sounds pretty suspicious."

"The investigator thought so, but that was where his investigation ended. He was more interested in the mechanics of the crash. It appears she had a worn brake line that was leaking brake fluid. He surmised that she had no brakes before the crash occurred."

"Worn brake line or severed?" he asked.

"Worn was his description. But the car was only just over a year old. He noted that as suspicious also."

"So, Angie was living on borrowed time anyway. If she had left the lab for a better paying job, she would have been killed to shut her up. Presumably."

"Presumably," she agreed.

"Honey, you did a fantastic job. I hope you didn't draw any attention to yourself doing it."

"Nope. I'm a professional busybody. Leave no trace, is my motto. And I'm that good. So you probably don't want to break up with me, or you'd be in real trouble."

"I'll keep that in mind," he laughed, although she did scare him a little. It was a good thing he planned on marrying her.

Chapter 6

The Articles

The news articles that Cindy had shown Steve began around 1975. Each one got stranger than the last. They were the type of articles that newspapers used as fillers, because they were too preposterous to be printed alongside real journalistic endeavors.

The first reported was the bald bear. A hairless bear was spotted in Rothrock State Forest in the summer of 1975. Of course, it was never reported as a bear.

A bear with no hair is a fearsome sight. It screams of being an otherworldly creature, because without its fur, it looks like nothing that the average person has ever seen before.

The original sighting had scared a group of hunters who were out rabbit hunting. They observed the bear feasting upon a dead deer.

Hairless bears do exist from time to time due to disease or conditions such as mange. What made this bear more frightening was that it was a genetically modified bear.

It had dined on a steady diet of growth hormones. It was a male black bear. Normally, a black bear tops out at six hundred pounds, and that would be a very large specimen.

The bear seen by the hunters was twelve hundred pounds and dwarfed the deer it was dining upon. To the three men interviewed for the article, it was an alien creature, not recognizable as a bear at all.

What added insult to injury was that the black bear's skin is actually gray. So they were observing a huge gray carnivorous beast, never seen by man before. Because of its unnatural size, that was a true statement.

It became known locally as Hellhound. And it was spotted from time to time by fishermen and hikers.

Four of the articles in Cindy's scrapbook dealt with the Hellhound specifically. The true nature of the beast was never discovered. The legend persists, even though the beast is long dead.

The steady diet of growth hormones cut the beast's average life span of twenty-five years down to twelve. The scientists learned quite a bit from the experiment. They considered it a success and cared not one bit about the stir it caused locally. It actually amused them so much that they began calling the poor beast Hellhound.

The scientists also were successful in raising badgers in the eighty to ninety-pound range. Badgers were considered huge if they reached thirty-five pounds in the wild. The problem was that they couldn't control them.

The badger needed no additional aggression training. A handler was eventually killed and that particular experiment was curtailed. Unfortunately, three of the beasts had tunneled out of captivity and roamed the countryside for about ten years. The normal life span should have been twenty to twenty-five years. Once again, the growth hormones had proven deadly.

While roaming free, the oversized beasts would attack anything that they perceived posed a threat. Luckily for the public, two of the beasts found each other threatening and fought to the death. Neither one survived.

The remaining badger took out a whole pack of hunting dogs and backed down only when the hunter, who owned the dogs, fired at it repeatedly.

The stories grew from there of the Devil Beast. Devil and Hell figure into a lot of the names. Apparently, that was considered a logical naming scheme for unexplainable and scary creatures.

The badger experiments started up once again in 2015, unbeknownst to anyone but employees and soldiers at the secret facility. Of course, no one knew about the original experiments, except those at the facility.

The most fanciful experiment involved trying to make a unicorn. The experiment was actually called, 'The Unicorn Project.'

The scientists tried to splice together the DNA of a horse and rhinoceros. It makes more sense than it sounds.

The horse and the rhino belong to the same group or family known as the Perissodactyls. The shared characteristics are that they are mammals, herbivores and they possess either one or three hoofed toes on each hindfoot.

The result was a sleeker, taller rhino. One of the beasts broke through a corral fence and roamed the countryside for weeks until the scientists figured out a way to lure it back home.

As luck would have it, it was spotted at least three times in its short bout of freedom. It was dubbed, 'The Horned Forest Monster.'

It was treated mostly as a joke by the press. It was first spotted by a bunch of pot smoking college students from Juniata College.

The second group to spot the creature was a group of hikers, and the third sighting was by a group of amateur bird enthusiasts.

Each time an article was printed with a humorous twist, which must have made the persons who reported it feel silly. If it had been seen by anyone else, they kept it to themselves for fear of ridicule.

Another series of articles were written about sasquatch sightings. This had nothing to do with the scientific experiments at the secret facility, but had the scientists in a tizzy.

They wanted a sasquatch more than anything. The potential in creating a sasquatch goon squad was exponential.

The articles had credibility because they spanned a period of fifty or more years. Many of those who reported sightings were credible individuals whom would have nothing to gain by making such a claim.

The scrapbook also claimed other oddities and strange sightings. It all added up to one thing: This little corner of Rothrock State Forest had exceeded its weirdness quotient.

And the only logical explanation was the secret facility.

Gladys stood on the back porch, "Daryl! Daryl! Come to momma, honey!"

These last two weeks had forged the most unusual bond in human history. Daryl had healed well, and his pain had dropped off considerably since befriending Gladys. And the big creature knew she had helped him considerably.

Today she had something special planned. Besides his allotment of beef, she had baked him two delicious apple pies. She had never made him sweets before, and she was eager to see his reaction.

Daryl strode through the forest quickly to get to his friend's abode. He loved having a friend. Her kindness had made his life so much better.

He entered her back yard. She was glad to see him as usual.

He stopped short of her porch and sniffed. The aroma was intoxicating. He didn't know what it was, but he hoped it was for him.

She pointed at the two oversized aluminum pie pans and said, "Pie, Daryl. Momma has baked you pies."

She held one out in front of him. He gently, always gently, took it from her. He held it up to his nose. He wanted to savor that smell first.

Gladys watched. She knew grown men who wouldn't have the brains to appreciate the smell. They would just wolf it down and want more.

Unfortunately, Mr. Bomberger was that way. He never appreciated the result of the art of baking. He'd slam down a piece of pie, and then ask if there was more. Not her Daryl. He was savoring every aspect of it.

When he began eating it, he took his time. He started making excited grunting sounds. And then he put his lips together and said, "Mmmmm."

Gladys was happier than she had been in years. Finally, someone who appreciated her baking, besides the rangers.

He saw how delighted she was by the noise he made. He repeated it, "Mmmmm." His humanity was showing.

Chapter 7

The Plan

The cloning of a sasquatch had never been tried before. Up to this point, the samples for DNA analysis had only been hair samples and some scat that was believed to be from the creature.

There was nothing viable to begin the process of cloning. But this hand was exactly what was needed.

The initial cloning would include absolutely no modifications. They knew nothing about the creature to even venture a guess for modification.

With mountain lions, bears, deer and even porcupines, the ideas for modifications were easy. There were a multitude of physical modifications and behavioral. Successes and failures were part of the process.

Sasquatches were a virtual unknown. The plan would be different in scope than any other plan they had devised.

They decided to clone three sasquatches.

Number One would be raised in virtual isolation. Food and aid would be supplied with no nurturing. The hope would be to raise a sasquatch as naturally as possible. Although, they had no idea what parenting skills the species supplied to its members. And truth be told, they weren't one hundred percent sure if sasquatches were solitary creatures or lived in small pods.

Number Two would be raised with nurturing and kindness from human beings. Guidance would be given to see how the creature would respond to training. It would receive the best care that they could supply.

Number Three would be mistreated to increase aggression. Withholding food and basic comforts would be part of the experiment. The team had successfully increased aggression in a whole host of other animals. They were quite skilled at the practice. Man's claim to fame is to have mastered cruelty.

Through the experiment, they would begin to learn how to make the beast malleable for use on the battlefield, especially in forested areas.

It was the age-old story of a twisted military complex looking for the most efficient killing machine.

They were prepared for setbacks as they learned the basic physiology of the creatures. The scientists were clueless as to longevity of the beast, what diseases affected them, what food sources may be harmful and whether they had any natural enemies in the wild.

The slate was blank. And even though they would clone a few sasquatches, they would never truly have the knowledge one gains from watching the actual creatures in the wild.

Right from the start, they would be interfering with the course of nature, but that was what man has always done. At least these men of letters already knew that. They had come to terms with their roles.

Steve, following his girlfriend's excellent research, became concerned that any further efforts on her part would lead to her being identified and considered a threat by those who killed Angie, and possibly Maxine.

He made her promise to cease her efforts, and she promised she would. The sasquatch's hand was gone. Steve had come to terms with that.

The worst part of the entire affair, besides Angie's murder, was notifying Scott and Ted Milburn that the hand had been lost. They were not happy.

Steve told them the series of event ending with Angie's murder, but never mentioned the top secret federal facility.

He warned the men that pursuing it further may have negative consequences.

When they asked who would want the sasquatch's hand so badly that they would kill for it, Steve had no answer. He held his tongue, in regards to implicating the federal government or the military.

The two men ended their encounter with Steve, feeling he was in on it and was as untrustworthy as anyone. Steve hated that. He had spent his entire career working hard to maintain integrity in his position with the public and the men and women whom worked for him.

After engaging the brothers, he truly let the sasquatch hand affair go. He had so much more to take care of. The police in State College would have to be left alone to do their job.

Sergeant Richard Krantz was the lead investigator on the Angela Summers case. Two weeks into the investigation, they had hit a dead end.

The parking garage had both still cameras at the exit gate and video security cameras on every level. What was discovered was the following:

Her murderer was a Caucasian male of medium height and medium build.

He drove a black BMW, but his license plate had been obscured.

He had taken what might have been the missing cryogenics transport unit from her back seat and put it into his own car in the back seat.

He and his car have disappeared.

No one knew what was in the cryogenics transport unit. A rumor suggested a piece of the mythological sasquatch was in the box.

Krantz was ready to dismiss the silly rumor, until he talked to Phil Snavely, the number two man at the lab. The sergeant determined that the man was not given to flights of fancy.

Although Snavely could not confirm the contents of the cryogenics unit, he alluded that a high ranking state ranger had thoughts on the issue and maybe he should be interviewed.

Krantz called Ranger Steve Brighton and made an appointment to see him.

When Steve received the call from Krantz, he was both surprised and angry.

Surprised, because anything he would have to say would be mostly hearsay. No hand means no proof.

He was also afraid he would have to involve the Milburn brothers, and they were already pissed and didn't trust him.

Angry, because he had decided to let this entire distasteful affair behind him. Now Krantz wanted to drag it out longer than it had to be.

On the day of the interview, Krantz arrived at the Raystown Lake Ranger Station. First blush revealed a man who was not physically impressive at all.

He was short and stocky with a bald head, black moustache and hands with plump sausage-like fingers. Steve wondered how the man ever passed his physical training to become a police officer.

Although uninvited, Krantz sat down in the chair across from Steve's desk and jumped right in with his questions.

"Phil Snavely has reason to believe that you think you know what was in the cryogenic box that was taken from Angela Summer's car. Is that true?"

Steve didn't like the man right from his first words, but they were both professionals. Steve wanted to help if he could.

"Phil is jumping to conclusions. All I can tell you about is my interaction with Angie shortly before she was killed."

"Don't keep me in suspense. Continue."

Steve bristled a bit at the man's rudeness.

"Two men brought a sample to me on the Tuesday before she died. I ran that sample up to her lab that same afternoon. I found out Thursday morning, from Phil, that she never entered the sample into the labs queue for testing."

"Why not?"

"How would I know? I gave it to her. Hell, I even bribed her with a bag of M&M's to be quick about it."

"You bribed her?"

"Yes. I asked her for favors and sometimes she attached gifts that she must receive before she would honor the favor. Never money, just things like candy or flowers. She was always flirting with me."

"And Cindy didn't mind?"

Steve was shocked. "How do you know my girlfriend's name?"

"I'm a cop. It's my job. Cindy didn't get jealous?" he persisted.

"No. I never told her. It was harmless flirting, and I always let Angela know I wasn't interested."

"Yes. Bringing a girl a bag of M&M's always sets the record straight," the detective deadpanned.

So the man had a dry sense of humor. If Steve hadn't already decided to dislike him, he might have actually learned to appreciate the man.

Krantz continued with his questions, "What was the nature of the sample you took to her?"

Steve sighed and thought, *here we go.* "It was the severed hand of what I believed to be a sasquatch."

Krantz just gave him a penetrating stare.

Finally, the detective asked, "You mean like a Bigfoot type creature?"

"Yes. It was at least three times the size of a human hand, but it had short fingers." Steve wanted to say, 'like yours,' but he controlled himself. "It had a very thick palm, the texture of sandpaper, and thick, ragged fingernails and hair on the back side of it."

"And that is what you claim was in the ice box she was carrying?"

"I have no idea what was in the cryogenic transport unit. I merely suggested to Phil, that since it had been live tissue, maybe she would use such a device to take it somewhere. But Phil insisted there was nowhere for her to take it. They didn't consult with others outside of the lab."

"Can anyone else verify the nature of your sample?" Krantz inquired.

Steve surprised him, "Yes, two men actually. Two brothers, Scott and Ted Milburn. I can call them and see if they can come over."

"Not necessary. Just give me their addresses. I'll talk to them separately."

"But I could call them and coach them before you ever got there," Steve pointed out.

Krantz stared at him once again and said, "Is that what you're going to do, Ranger Brighton?"

"No," Steve said rather sheepishly.

"Good. I have all I need from you, except the Milburn brothers' addresses."

Steve gave it to him and was glad he was gone. He was as creepy as anything Steve had read about in Cindy's scrapbook.

Chapter 8

Six Months Later

Doctor Nolte was the scientific lead on the project. Six months had passed and General Wartman wanted an update so that he in turn could report to his superiors at the Pentagon and in Congress.

Nolte began, while Dougherty and Ganse looked on respectfully. The team had made some amazing headway and couldn't wait to share it.

"Let me start by saying the new synthesized growth hormone is safer than any version we have tried yet. The risk to the test subjects has been minimal," Nolte announced.

"Good. How long will one of these things live?" the General asked.

"We couldn't tell you, General," Nolte replied nervously, "because this is a new species to us. We have no knowledge of their normal or standard longevity. We just know, because we're monitoring via blood tests, that we are being minimally invasive with our drugs."

General Wartman nodded for him to continue.

"Clone A, the one that has been isolated and interfered with the least, has grown to over five feet and weighs over three hundred and fifty pounds.

"He has become a master of concealment and his strength for his size is impressive. Psychologically, he shows signs of extreme shyness and bouts of psychosis.

"He, at times, appears unaware we are present, even when we make ourselves known. Normally, he would hide and observe us, but a few times he has appeared to be communicating with a non-existent entity."

"You mean God?" the General asked.

"No, sir. More like an imaginary playmate. Like a child would invent. He is, after all, a toddler that has had his lifetime accelerated. It may have caused the psychotic breaks that we have observed."

"Continue," the military man instructed.

"Clone B has been a delight. We have spared no nurturing opportunity. For all practical purposes, he thinks he is a human child. He has bonded closely with his handlers, Bob and Linda, and sees them as his parents.

"The beast has formed a loving relationship with them and seeks their approval at every turn, making him extremely susceptible to receiving and following instructions," Nolte stated proudly.

"Great! You're raising an ape child. Will he kill for them if pressed?" asked the General.

"We don't know, sir. That wasn't part of this experiment. Maybe Clone C will be more to your liking," Nolte suggested.

"Get to it, Doctor."

"Clone C is a killer. It performs basic tasks to receive food and favors. We have purposely designed its upbringing to make it aggressive. And we have been extremely successful.

"It also is the largest and heaviest of the three. It stands almost six feet tall and weighs in at about four hundred pounds. And that is with a very restricted diet, which is part of the aggression training."

"Is it controllable?" the General asked.

"Under the right conditions, yes," Nolte stated.

"And what might those conditions be, Doctor? We want a sasquatch soldier. A soldier obeys commands. Can you get there with this animal?"

"I believe we can, General. But it is extremely early in the life of the experiment. We were to have a minimum of three years to fully habituate the clones to our manipulation and interference," Nolte explained.

"Three years," grumbled the General. "Look at me, Doctor. I'm not a young man anymore. Three years is significant when you get to be my age. I want reportable results earlier than that!"

"Then Clone C is the one we will concentrate on. He has already injured two handlers. He's angry and faster than you can imagine. We will work on his ability to be manipulated in the field. I have a few ideas that may work, that we haven't yet tried."

Doctor Dougherty became a bit concerned at this modification to the experiment on the fly, for the impatient General's sake, "What did you have in mind, Doctor Nolte?"

"Aversion therapy might suit that beast very well," Nolte noted.

"But Doctor, it could actually make him hyper aggressive. That would be counter to what the General actually wants," Dougherty pointed out.

The General stood up and said, "You girls fight this out among yourselves. I've got things to do." He then walked out of the meeting.

Nolte was fuming, "Don't ever question me like that in front of the General! We must present a united front. He is too volatile to deal with. He could shut this experiment down on a whim! Next time, Dougherty, keep your questions for our private meetings!"

Nolte stormed out of the room, much like the General had done.

Dougherty and Ganse didn't like the way things were going. Nolte was as volatile as he had just warned them that the General could be.

Gladys and Daryl sat in the back yard. It was warm for a spring day. She was sitting in a lawn chair knitting a scarf.

Daryl was dining on thirty pounds of steak. She had another half side of beef being delivered in two days. Feeding him was very expensive, but her husband had a rather large insurance policy when he died.

She had no other expenses, except for fuel oil in the winter and her property taxes, which were negligible. No children were waiting for a large inheritance.

She thought about it and realized that Daryl was the closest thing to family that she had. Gladys did have a niece in Indiana, but their only contact was a Christmas card in December. She also received a birthday card in February, and she would in turn send one in June, which was her niece's birth month. The relationship wasn't exactly dripping with sentiment, visits or phone calls.

Mr. Bomberger had a brother in a nursing home somewhere, but she couldn't remember the location. He actually may be dead by now. She had no way of knowing. Nor did she really care.

Daryl was here. He was gentle and faithful. She fed him and in return he listened to her talk. She had also taught him a few words.

The most important word was *danger*. When she said that word, he jumped up and ran into the woods. She would say it when the fuel oil man would come and also the butcher's van when it delivered her side of beef.

She was very protective of her new friend. She didn't need to call the rangers anymore so that she would have someone to talk to. They just wanted her cookies and pies anyway.

Speaking of pies, she would bake Daryl two pies, once a week. He loved his sweets. He had gotten to the point of making a real melodramatic show of saying *Mmmmm* in appreciation. It warmed her heart and made her laugh.

He was such a sweet boy.

She wished she knew more about his kind. She had gone to the library and found some horror books that made sasquatches sound like bloodthirsty murderers. She didn't bother reading those. She knew the truth was just the opposite.

Daryl farted.

That she could do without. When her sweet Daryl passed gas, it was enough to gag a maggot, as Mr. Bomberger used to say.

Apparently, his digestive system turned beef into poison gas. She had shown such disdain for his nasty habit that he usually stood up and went to the tree line when he felt he was working one up.

One night as it was getting late, Gladys accidently farted. It was loud and Daryl wasn't going to let it go unnoticed. He stood up, howled and pretended to drop over dead.

She laughed for twenty minutes before finally telling him goodnight. Then she went in the house and laughed for another twenty minutes.

Her sweet Daryl was the light of her life.

Chapter 9

One Year into the Experiment

The General sat at the head of the table. His countenance was stern. He wanted results. One year of his life was invested in these sasquatch clones, and he wanted something positive to report to his superiors.

"Doctor Nolte, thrill me," he commanded.

"The shock collar is working. Clone C hates it and will do almost anything to avoid it being employed," Nolte reported.

"Excuse me, Doctor. Didn't you tell me three months ago the shock collar wasn't working?" the General reminded him.

"Yessir, that is correct. It just wasn't strong enough to get his attention. The new collar makes his eyes roll back in his head. He's onboard now."

Dougherty and Ganse looked on silently as usual. There was a disagreement among the three. Dougherty and Ganse felt it was a poor way to get a creature to do a specific task.

The sasquatch had to be monitored constantly while in the field. It liked to attempt to catch its handlers off guard. The supposition was that if it caught them with their guard down, it would kill them to avoid being shocked. It was not a good situation, but Doctor Nolte preferred to ignore the problem, so he could please the General.

Clone A was euthanized. The psychotic breaks it suffered became a permanent condition. It became completely divorced from the real world.

It was determined that whatever parenting and nurturing a mother sasquatch supplied was necessary for the creature to function normally. But that was a guess.

The comparison with Clone B determined that the humans had taken the place of a sasquatch parent. And as far as Clone C, it was determined that even negative parenting and abuse was preferable to no parenting at all.

Clone B was still working out well. It had basically become a pet. One point of concern was highlighted by the one time that Clone C saw Clone B. It went berserk and tried to get to Clone B, presumably to kill it. The reaction was totally unexpected and unexplainable.

Three more clones were in the tubes. Clones A and C were males, but B was a female. She was, of course, sterile, but still had a womb to implant a new clone. The doctors had changed the clone at the chromosomal level. She was true female, but her sterility was taking place at conception. With a balanced hormone treatment, she would be able to give birth to implanted clone cells. At least that was the theory.

The scientists would be able to learn much about the natural gestation period of the sasquatch, if a viable clone cluster could be successfully implanted.

Clone B was very healthy and now stood six feet, ten inches tall. She weighed in at six hundred pounds. She was a formidable mammal.

Clone C, however, was a beast to be reckoned with. At seven foot, seven inches and weighing seven hundred and sixty pounds, he struck fear into all who saw him, including his handlers.

When deployed in the field for testing, a team of five men were assigned to him. Two held the controls to his shock collar, one carried a tranquilizer rifle and two had tranquilizer pistols.

The darts in the tranquilizer were filled with a five milligram dose of the animal tranquilizer, Carfentanil. It is one of the most powerful and fast-acting tranquilizers ever developed. It could take down a bull, a buffalo or even a small elephant.

The General addressed a rumor that he had heard, "Doctor Nolte, I've heard something disturbing. Is it true that it takes five men to go out with the beast during training?"

"Yessir. Why is that disturbing?" Nolte asked.

"You don't get it, do you? We want to put killer sasquatches in the field, to replace using men. Saving the lives of our own soldiers is at the heart of these endeavors, but if we have to put five men at risk just to deploy one sasquatch, we've failed," the General declared, being overly dramatic.

Nolte had enough, "This is year one of a three year experiment. It'll take at least three years, and I don't care how old you are! Science takes time and shouldn't be rushed!"

This was the first time Nolte had ever pushed back.

"Take it easy, Doc. Just try to get it down to one handler per biological vertebrate weapon," the General informed him and left the meeting.

Ganse finally broke his silence, "Biological vertebrate weapon? Is that our new term for our test subjects?"

"He's the General. If that is what he wants to call them, then fine. I'm thinking we should terminate Clone C and start from scratch," Nolte suggested.

"I concur. The damn thing scares me half to death," Dougherty added his consent.

Ganse affirmed the idea as well.

It was settled. When the beast returned from its current training exercise, they would tranquilize the sasquatch and give it an overdose of a powerful sedative.

Cindy was the one to remind him, "You know, this is the anniversary of Angie Summer's death."

"Well, for a fiancé, you're kind of ghoulish. Had I known you kept track of things like that, I may not have asked you to marry me."

"Oh, relax. It was on the front page of the Centre Daily Times. It was pointing out that no headway has been made in the case. Don't you find that odd?"

"No. If it was the government that snuffed the poor girl, then they would make sure it was never solved. Just forget it. We no longer have any connection to the case, the sasquatch hand or anything else. We're just two people headed towards marital bliss," he declared emphatically.

"You're really not curious? The facility is in your state forest," she reminded him.

"Not interested in the least. I have too many parks and forests that need my attention. And the spring brings out all the nuts with rifles. Soon my hands will be full of boaters and those hunters with bloodlust coursing through their veins. I don't need any other distractions, except you."

"I was just wondering if we should go upstairs and get distracted for a while?" she suggested as a cute question.

"I have a quarterly payroll report to do. So, my God, yes. Distract me."

She ran up the steps. He followed just as quickly.

Ranger Milt Cox walked out of the Marine Sales showroom. He had just placed a down payment on his dream.

He and his wife were doing great. They were leaving on a cruise in three weeks. Everything was going well at work too. He had just gotten his yearly raise on his anniversary date with the State Ranger Service.

He couldn't imagine anything going wrong. The spring was when things became a bit busier. That would just mean that the three weeks prior to the cruise would go by more quickly.

Ranger Tom Deering had made it a habit to drop in on Gladys every now and again. She sometimes seemed friendly and sometimes perturbed. In that way, the old woman reminded him of his mother.

He noticed that she kept him confined to the front of the house and away from the windows looking into the back yard. He assumed she didn't want to talk about the sasquatch.

As long as she was healthy and was willing to treat him to chocolate chip cookies, he was fine. He wouldn't be able to check on her as much. Warm spring days were going to keep him busy with the increase in people flowing into the Raystown Lake Recreation Area.

He kept her Polaroid for himself. Steve had said not to go public. He pointed out that every nut in Pennsylvania, Maryland and Ohio would flood the area looking for sasquatches.

He saw his point as a good one. It was enough that they knew the truth. He hadn't even shared it with his wife, Linda.

As of late, unfortunately, he and Linda were not sharing much. She had grown distant, or maybe he had. Fifteen years of marriage is a long time.

He worked a lot. She had a job as well, at the bank. She, of course, had banker's hours, and he worked the second shift quite often. He wanted to fix things, but didn't know how. She didn't seem bothered by their current situation.

Life was strange. At least he loved his job. That would never change. There would be plenty of time for he and Linda to get things back on track.

Ranger Tom Bollman continued to run into rough characters that insisted on doing things the hard way. Some he would turn away, having taught them a lesson, and others he arrested because he knew they would hurt other people for sport. He had a knack for being able to read people fairly well.

Other than Steve, he was the ranger most skilled at handling aggressive and uncooperative people. He seemed to be a magnet for them. When stories were shared about how their week had gone, he would always reveal how he had to deal with what he called, 'the hard cases,' almost twice as much as the others.

He was a handsome man, but not physically imposing. He stood at only five foot ten inches, and he weighed in at one hundred and eighty pounds.

He knew that didn't make him a shrimp, by any means, but his size just didn't command authority. People always felt the need to challenge him, much to their dismay.

He thought it funny, because after his boxing days, he had considered the priesthood. He was generally a very peaceful soul. His education would have served him well in that position.

The reason he didn't become a priest was named Darcy. They had been married for three years and had a little boy named Zach. He loved them with every fiber of his being.

His life was going the way he wanted on almost every front. Being a ranger had never really been part of his plan at any point. But the job was available and he met the qualifications, so he applied. And here he was.

If he really was able to pick what he wanted to do, it would be to make and sell furniture. He was an extremely talented woodworker. It might have been another reason he didn't enter the priesthood. He was afraid he would have to give it up, and it was the one piece of his father that he had left.

His mother had died at an early age, and his father was currently in an Alzheimer's unit in Huntingdon. They had spent most of his childhood making furniture together.

His father's pieces were in the homes of many wealthy people. He was that good.

Tom was thinking about his father when he saw the old man, fishing alone, along the shore of the creek at the base of the bridge that he was crossing. It reminded him of the other thing that he and his dad had shared many hours doing together.

Tom was just in a sad place on this particular day. His father's condition was weighing on his mind. Whenever he got like this, he simply counted his blessings and that would usually drive away his funk.

Overall, life was good.

Chapter 10

Awry

Jim Samson was the one carry the tranquilizer rifle today. And even armed with that gun didn't make him feel safe. He hated the beast, and the beast hated everybody.

He needed to try to keep the creature in sight at all times. Right now, Kong was missing from his view and he didn't like it. They had started calling the thing Kong, after King Kong. Calling it Clone C became tiresome.

Where in the hell are you, big buddy? Samson thought to himself. "Martin, Rico, do either of you see him? I've lost him," Jim reported to the team. Martin and Rico held the shock controls.

"We don't see him either. Tim, Ron, how about you guys? All I hear is some kind of clicking." Martin responded.

"We don't see the son of a bitch either. Shock him so he makes some noise. We'll follow the growling and whimpering," Ron suggested.

Alone in the shadows, Kong picked up a rock. He knew it might hurt, but he didn't care. He slammed the rock into his own throat hitting the shock collar. He repeated the action over and over.

After the eleventh hit, it fractured. On the twelfth hit, it loosened. And luckily for Kong, on the thirteenth, it fell to the ground.

Kong rubbed his neck. It hurt, but not as bad as the collar. He bent over, picked it up and growled quietly.

Now the game begins.

Martin pressed the button on the controller in his left hand. He listened. Nothing.

He repeated the sequence. Nothing

"Rico, try your controller. Mine isn't working."

Rico tried it, as requested. Nothing. Just as Martin had done, he repeated the actions. Nothing.

"Pull your weapons, gentlemen. The collar doesn't seem to be working. I'll call for reinforcements," Rico informed them.

Martin heard the crack of a twig behind him. He swung around, still holding the shock controller. Kong stood looking at him.

His thumb began pumping the button frantically.

Kong held up the collar between two fingers while maintaining eye contact with Martin.

Martin Best couldn't believe what he was seeing. *Is he actually smiling at me?* was the last living thought Martin had.

One down.

Rico tried over and over to get someone to respond to him on the radio handset. Panic was beginning to set in. He knew they needed help and fast.

Rico heard a scream off to his left. He knew it was Tim Garcia. It wasn't a scream for help, but a cry of agony.

Two down.

Jim caught up with Ron, "That was Tim! I just know it was! Have you seen Kong? Why aren't the collar pushers making him scream out?"

Ron said, "Calm down. We still have our tranq guns. He's a stupid animal. I know we can handle this."

Both men screamed at the same time, as Kong jumped out of the shadows. He towered over them.

Jim turned to run, but was stopped by a huge hand grabbing the top of his head and twisting violently. His neck snapped, and he was released to drop to the ground, totally devoid of feeling from the neck down.

As Kong repeatedly slammed Ron up against a tree, Jim suffocated to death, as his brain could not communicate to his diaphragm and the external intercostal muscles that he needed to breath.

Four down.

Rico finally raised a secretary. He was put on hold as she went to get someone, 'who knows what to do.' Right then, he knew that he was screwed.

Kong sniffed the air. The beast couldn't count, in the conventional sense, but he knew there was one left to be eliminated. He strained to catch the scent.

Rico saw one option. If the others were already neutralized, he needed to go up. He scanned the trees around him and saw one that would do nicely. He ran over to it and began to climb.

It was good that he acted upon his idea with urgency. Less than a minute after he began his climb, Kong was at the base of the tree and looking up.

The sasquatch had tremendous upper body strength, but its height to weight ratio made climbing a tree prohibitive. The lower branches may provide support, but very quickly the branches would prove to be inadequate.

Rico looked down into the eyes of the Devil himself. The stare was the most malevolent stare that Rico had ever seen. The monster kept rubbing his throat where the collar had been. Rico wondered how he removed it.

He could only hope that they would be missed and help would be on its way. But he knew that if help did arrive, chances were that they would be unprepared for what awaited them.

At least he was safe, so he thought.

The first rock hit the branch above him, and he felt the vibrations. The second rock hit his branch, only inches from his left hand. The branch literally shook from the blow.

He looked down in time to see Kong launch the rock that knocked him loose from his perch. He fell, hitting four branches on the way down and landed broken and bleeding at the base of the tree.

Kong loomed over him. The beast lifted his huge foot and brought it down quickly.

Five down.

There was no one left to prevent Kong from going wherever he wanted. And he knew it.

The General hounded the secretary to remember Rico's exact words. The poor woman was pushed to tears. The General felt no remorse. Weakness was the most unattractive quality that a human being could display.

Rico didn't answer on the radio. The General sent out three squads of professional soldiers which was every available soldier he had.

They were heavily armed. There were no tranquilizer guns for this mission. They carried automatic weapons using 5.56mm rounds. Clone C was to be put down.

The men were divided into three lethal units. They scoured the area and found their first dead comrade after forty-five minutes. Three hours later, they had located all five dead handlers and the broken shock collar.

What they didn't locate was Clone C. Kong had escaped. They had never implanted a tracking device under his skin because the tracking device had been incorporated into his collar.

The three doctors sat with the General. Nolte was the one to make the mistake, "General, we need to notify the local authorities. This isn't like the other specimens that have escaped. This one is a killer, with no off switch. Even we can't hide behind our secrecy on this one."

The General stood up and first glared at Nolte and then at the other two. The doctors were frightened by his look.

"Gentlemen," the General began, "people have died to protect the secrecy of this facility. Three more deaths will not make much of a difference. Have I made myself clear?"

Doctor Nolte answered for himself and his colleagues, "Crystal, General. We understand. Will you continue to neutralize the threat?"

"Only if we can find it! We'll have to wait and watch. You three need to continue with your experiments. I'll handle Clone C."

They agreed and left the room. The General picked up the phone and called his superiors in Washington.

Chapter 11

The First Incident

Tyke Gillespie was an avid fisherman. He had come in second, first and second respectively in the lake fishing tournament the last three years.

Everyone in the area knew Tyke, and almost all who knew him liked him. He was a beloved character known for his kindness, helpfulness and a pretty good sense of humor.

He was always a gentleman around the ladies, and a good friend to those who were down on their luck. He volunteered at the local food bank and was a deacon in his church.

Tyke was the kind of citizen that every small town needed to keep its character flourishing and its history alive. He was a retired used car salesman, but instead of his customers having bad stories about dishonesty and craftiness, his customers could only speak of his forthrightness and willingness to help people afford to own a car. They would always purchase a good used vehicle that wouldn't let them down.

If Tyke would have run for president, he would have had every vote in Huntingdon and the surrounding area.

As much as he loved people, he loved the solitude that fishing afforded him. To him, sitting on the bank of a lake or a creek drowning worms was his idea of heaven.

He also was equally happy on his bass boat which he named, appropriately, *My Retirement*. Today he was sitting in his boat and casting for striped bass.

His lure box was the size of a small suitcase. He joked that he had two of every lure ever made. The only thing he was more passionate about than fishing were his grandkids.

He had three grandsons. One was at West Point, one at Annapolis and the one in Colorado Springs wanted to fly jets. His two granddaughters were no slouches either. One was in her third year of medical school and the other had just qualified for the Women's Olympic Ski Team.

He often wondered how a used car salesman could possibly have given rise to such successful and motivated progeny. He was proud of them twenty-four hours a day.

His son and daughter were no slouches either. Neil was a senior vice president in a regional bank and Lilah was a nursing supervisor at Wills Eye Hospital in Philadelphia.

Sometimes when thinking of how successful his family had become, melancholy set in. Marie would have been so proud of all of them. His wife died seven years ago from cervical cancer.

It made him sad that she had missed so much of her hard work paying off. She was an excellent mother, and as far as Tyke was concerned, a better woman had never walked the face of the earth.

When he thought that thought, he always asked Jesus to forgive him. And then he would say aloud, "Your mother not included, Lord."

Using different jigs wasn't helping much today. Nothing was biting. After a bit, he just settled on drifting along the shore. It was a beautiful, warm spring day and he was enjoying the alone time.

At noon, he opened his lunchbox. He had made himself two ham and cheese sandwiches on potato bread, a bag of potato chips and two huge chocolate chip cookies. The cookies weren't store bought. The cookies were made from Marie's favorite Toll House recipe. Her oversized cookies were the kids' favorite. He continued the tradition, not only for himself, but his grandkids as well.

His boat was lazily drifting, and he was thinking random thoughts when he saw a sudden movement along the shore at the tree line. He squinted, trying to focus in on what had caught his attention.

It was big, so he assumed a deer had come to the lake's edge for a drink. He was in a good spot to take the boat onto shore and jump off.

Once the front of the boat rested in the soft mud, he walked to the front and jumped off. He walked close to the tree line and peered into the darkened forest.

He held two pieces of bread from one of his sandwiches. Tyke had coaxed deer to eat from his hand many times before. They had a natural curiosity that drew them in. He was hoping it wouldn't be too shy today.

It stepped out in front of him.

Steve picked up the phone. It was almost four in the afternoon.

"Ranger Brighton, this is Billy Hayes from the Raystown Lake Tour Boat company. One of my boats just found Tyke Gillespie's bass boat adrift along the eastern shore.

"Tyke wasn't on it. I'm afraid there may have been an accident of some kind."

"Where is the boat now?" Steve asked.

"One of my boys went aboard and dropped anchor, in case that particular spot was important. They also launched the dinghy from the tour boat, and one of them stayed in the area to look around. The tour continued, so he's still out there with the boat."

"Thank you, Billy. Do you have any other craft that could head out that way?" Steve asked.

"Sorry, Ranger Brighton. Skeleton crew."

"Okay. Thanks again."

The call ended and Steve called Milt Cox. He told him to head to the marina and to fire up the ranger's boat.

The Raystown Ranger Station had a mini tugboat assigned to the lake. It came in handy in many situations. This was one of them.

He then called Tom Bollman in off patrol. Tom Deering was off today. He tasked Tom with gathering some volunteers and walking the eastern shoreline.

Steve knew Tyke Gillespie well. The circumstances told him one thing. Unless Tyke had somehow made it to shore, this would not be a rescue, but rather a recovery.

The thought saddened him. He headed for the marina.

Kong's appetite was sated. The weak one had come along at just the right time. The beast had been famished.

Having just ate his fill, he moved along slowly. He observed the weak creatures on the lake, riding on what he was unsure. The things they rode upon were all shapes and sizes. This was all new to him.

He walked along the eastern shore tree line, careful to not be observed.

He suddenly stopped and sniffed the air.

The scent was faint, but familiar. His mind could not readily identify what it was, but he knew the direction from whence it came and headed that way.

The smell made him feel agitated. His primitive, aggressive mind wanted to smash whatever it was.

Kong didn't like heading towards the unknown scent and feeling like he was preparing for a fight. The unknown caused him fear. And he didn't like being afraid at all.

The ranger's tug was working the area around the anchored bass boat. A few private vessels had joined them. Many of the men in the boats had been friends of Tyke's.

The trek along the eastern shore had been going on for forty minutes or so. Steve could see the line of volunteers in the distance being led by Ranger Bollman.

They had one hour of daylight left, at best. From what Steve could tell, Tyke had just begun to eat his lunch. There was a bit of strangeness to what he found.

The contents of a ham and cheese sandwich lay on his cleaning table. The bread was missing. A second sandwich lay there, still in its Ziploc plastic bag. Two cookies were also similarly bagged, and an open bag of Utz potato chips lay there, seemingly untouched.

So what would have caused him to fall overboard. His poles were pulled in and stowed, unless there was a pole unaccounted for that may have fallen into the water.

There were no fish in the live well. His huge box of lures lay opened and ready for service at a moment's notice. *The man had a shitload of lures, that's for sure*, Steve thought to himself.

There was no sign of anything out of place, except the missing bread. Tyke's body was nowhere in sight.

Steve's radio crackled.

"Bollman to Brighton. Over."

"Go ahead. Over."

"We believe we found him. Over."

"What do you mean, you believe you found him? You know what he looks like. Over."

"I'm waving my arms so you can see where we are. I don't believe any more should be said over the air. Over"

"I see you. Cox and I will be right there. Over."

Tom grabbed his bullhorn, "You guys keep looking, while we have daylight left. We need to see something on shore." The volunteers in the boats waved their acknowledgement.

Cox steered the tug towards the shore. Steve grabbed a pair of hip waders so he could get to shore without getting soaked.

Milt got them within a few feet of the shoreline. It was a shallow area. Steve climbed over the back of the boat and dropped into about fourteen inches of water. He slogged the few feet to dry land.

"What do you have, Tom?"

As Steve walked towards Tom, he read the faces of the volunteers. It wasn't good.

One volunteer turned and started to gag..

Steve stood next to Tom. What he was seeing didn't make any sense. The first question he asked Tom was, "Did you find any bread?"

Chapter 12

The Bread

Steve had spent over an hour debriefing the land volunteers. He first had Milt go out and dismiss the boat volunteers. He tied the bass boat to the back of the tug, and towed it back over to shore.

The men whom had seen the remains of Tyke Gillespie were traumatized. Many of the men had seen combat in Vietnam, Iraq and Afghanistan and yet still found reason to be greatly disturbed.

The remains were identified on scene by Steve, pulling the poor man's wallet from the back pocket of his jeans. Someone else identified a tattoo on his left forearm of the four stars of the Southern Cross, representing the 23rd Infantry Division in Vietnam.

There was no doubt whom they were placing in the body bag. Whatever had attacked him had bitten and savaged the man's face. It was obvious that large chunks of Tyke's torso had been eaten.

Part of Steve's debriefing was spent trying to get the men from jumping to conclusions, although he couldn't blame them. They were torn between whether this was a ravenous bear that maybe woke up from hibernation or a mountain lion with a taste for human flesh.

Steve begged them to allow his people and the medical examiner to do their jobs and nail down what the culprit had been. All they could agree upon was that it sure as hell was no accident.

Steve sat with Milt and Tom Bollman, in their office, after ten at night.

Tom was dying to ask, so he did, "Why did you ask me about the bread?"

"It was right there, wasn't it?" Steve asked.

"Yes. It was completely out of place. A horribly mangled body on the ground. And three feet away, two slices of bread with one bite taken out of each. So, boss, what do you think happened?"

"I saw the ham and cheese that belonged to that bread. It was just one bite. I think Tyke had just begun to eat his lunch near the shore. My guess, he saw something on shore and misidentified it. He thought it was going to be cute and fuzzy and like bread, but it wasn't."

"But his boat was off shore. How do you explain that?" Milt asked.

"That one is simple. He brought it into shore close enough to jump off. Then sometime after he was dead, one of our speed-freak motorboat operators created a wake that moved it shoreward, raised the boat, turned it, and then it drifted to where it was found."

"Yep. Makes perfect sense. But which do you think did it, bear or big cat?" Milt asked.

Tom and Milt waited for Steve's answer.

Steve thought for a moment, "Maybe neither. I have only heard of two animals that would purposely destroy a human face like that: a dog or chimpanzee. In both cases, those animals know attacking the face makes it personal."

"Holy shit!" Tom said. "You think we have a wolf or a big coyote?"

Milt added, "Maybe a feral dog. It is possible."

"What? You discounting the chimpanzee?" Steve asked. "Me too. But a single coyote wouldn't have done that much damage. And it's doubtful for a wolf, too. But a pair or a pack, now that's possible."

"Too bad it was far enough from the water that it was all dry ground. Prints would have been nice," Tom added.

"Well, like I told the volunteers, let the medical examiner tell us conclusively what we need to look for. Right now, we need to call it a day."

No one argued. Tomorrow would come fast enough.

The medical examiner's name was Doctor David Pinkerton. He normally would be home watching his favorite shows at this time of night.

What was different was a case that had been brought in to be examined. A man had been partially eaten, and the local rangers wanted to know for what to be searching.

What the doctor determined was that the man had indeterminate wounds. There were bite radii that didn't match anything with which he was familiar.

The marks were vaguely humanlike, but much too large. And the tearing of much of the tissue was consistent, not with an animal biting and pulling, but rather, an actual ripping motion. And the good doctor knew of nothing that strong to cause such damage.

He sat at his desk, wondering what he was going to tell the rangers, when he heard a knock at the back door of the examination theater. He got up and removed a loaded pistol from his desk drawer.

"Who's there?" he asked through the door.

"Homeland Security, Doctor Pinkerton."

"What do you want?"

"We need to talk about the body you are examining tonight."

That was creepy, Pinkerton thought. *How do they know what I'm doing here?*

"Doctor, I'm texting my credentials to your phone," the disembodied voice announced.

Creepy again. How do they know my private number? he thought for the second time.

A text message alert went off on his cellphone. He removed his phone from his pocket. A clear photo ID of the man on the other side of the door appeared.

It didn't make him feel any safer.

"How do I know this is legit?"

The door burst in and knocked him to the floor. He raised his pistol, but was shot three times before he could defend himself.

One of the men bent over and picked up his phone, turned it off and pocketed the device.

The other two men erased the doctor's notes from his computer, which fortunately for them was still open to those same notes.

He had a micro recorder by the table. They took that and then collected the remains that the doctor had been examining.

All this occurred in less than four minutes.

On the way out, one man couldn't resist putting a bullet in the doctor's forehead.

They were gone.

Gladys sat rocking and watching her shows. Daryl had mended so well from his accident. He was getting quite adept at doing almost everything with one hand.

Their friendship had become the most important thing in her life. He was proving to be a better companion than Mr. Bomberger had been near the end of his life.

He seemed to appreciate every little thing she did for him. And he was so sweet. He tried to repay her, and that was awkward at first.

With one hand, he would catch animals and bring them to her so she could eat them with him. She got him to understand that she needed people food.

He purposely cut down on eating the beef. that she supplied for him. He supplemented her beef with the animals that he caught and she refused to eat.

When he saw her gardening and moving anything even slightly heavy, he would jump in to help. She couldn't even get her husband to do that on his best day.

They spent almost every afternoon and early evening sitting together. She took advantage of that opportunity to teach him some more words.

His diction wasn't the greatest, but he could say *beef, pie, flower, eat* and *ranger,* which rhymed with danger and always caused him to run into the woods. There were a few other words as well.

He was so much smarter than she had hoped he'd be. Her pet sasquatch was working out wonderfully. She loved him, and she was convinced that in his own way, he loved her too.

Life was good.

Things were about to change.

Chapter 13

The Missing Remains

Steve started his day by calling the medical examiner's office. He needed to formulate a plan to capture and euthanize whatever creatures that have become man killers.

The phone rang twice and was picked up, "Sergeant Willard, Pennsylvania State Police. How may I help you?"

"This is Ranger Steve Brighton, Raystown Lake Ranger Station. Since when do the state police answer the phone at the MEs office?"

"Since there was an incident here late last night that we're currently investigating. How may I help you, ranger?"

"I have a great need to speak to Doctor Pinkerton."

"I'm sorry. It isn't possible," the policeman told him.

"Officer, it is actually a matter of life and death," Steve persisted.

"How so, ranger?"

"We had a man badly mauled and killed yesterday. We need Doctor Pinkerton to tell us what we are looking for."

"Sorry, ranger. I feel for you, but you're not getting any help from Pinkerton today."

"Officer, just five minutes is all I need."

"Ranger Brighton, please keep this to yourself---one law enforcement professional to another. Doctor Pinkerton is dead. He was murdered last night." The Sergeant could see the caller ID was identifying the caller as calling from the ranger station. He took a chance.

"How?" Steve asked.

"He was shot several times. Once right in the middle of his forehead. He obviously was not meant to survive. I'm sorry. He won't be able to help you."

"Officer, can I talk to one of his assistants?"

"No, sorry. They are currently being interviewed and consoled, for that matter. The people here are pretty upset."

"Sergeant Willard, finding the answers I need may save someone's life. Please help me here."

"Ranger Brighton, I was charged to determine what was taken here, if anything. What we have determined is that Pinkerton's phone is missing and a body was taken. A Tyke Gillespie's remains are missing."

"You must be shitting me!" Steve said aloud, but hadn't meant to. "I'm sorry, Sergeant. I'm just shocked. I will let you go so you can get back to your crime scene. I appreciate you sharing things with me. I'll keep it quiet."

He was surprised that the policeman shared so much, but he was glad he did. Maybe he was hoping Steve would provide a motive or a clue.

Steve hung up as the blood drained from his face. He had just made a connection. A bullet to the middle of the forehead. It sounded very similar to Angela Summers' murder.

Could this be happening again? he thought. A missing sasquatch hand and a lab director's murder. A dead medical examiner and missing remains which were obviously from an animal attack.

What could it mean? They were too similar to not have a connection.

A thought struck him that seemed out of character with his normal pragmatic thought processes. *What if Tyke Gillespie was attacked by a sasquatch?*

The scent was getting stronger. Kong was becoming more confused and agitated. He traveled on.

Hunger was rearing its ugly head again. Kong was beginning to make finding food a bigger priority.

He sniffed the air, this time for food, not for the agitating odor that had him traveling in this direction. He smelled something that caused instant salivation. That was the smell for which he needed to find the source.

When he found the source of the maddening aroma, he stopped and observed.

Three campers, two women and one man, were frying bacon over an open fire. A large Igloo ice chest stood beside the fire. A carton of eggs was perched on top.

A large twelve foot by twelve foot tent was their backdrop. They were three friends just getting away for a quiet weekend.

The man was the boyfriend of one of the women, and the other woman was his younger sister. They had left their cellphones in their nearby Hyundai Sante Fe.

No screens was the theme of their outing. This was the second day of their vacation, and they all agreed they didn't miss their phones or computers at all.

The younger sister's boyfriend was to join them today. He would arrive after lunch.

"That bacon is driving me crazy. Hurry up and make those eggs!" the girlfriend playfully demanded.

"Oh, listen to Miss Model Perfect over here. You eat like a bird to stay thin and keep my brother interested. What are you going to do? Chow down on one whole piece of bacon?"

The girlfriend stuck her tongue out at the sister and then said, "I might pig out on two whole pieces. So there!"

The three laughed. They truly enjoyed each other's company. The running joke between the women was which couple was going to marry first. Both men were slow movers. How slow? The two women described them as glacially slow. That always engendered a round of laughter.

"Getting ready to start the eggs," the brother announced. "Leave your fat fingers off the bacon until it's ready."

"Okay," the girlfriend responded. "We'll take our fat fingers over to the water can and freshen up. Come on, Lisa."

Good, he thought, *I hate people hanging around waiting and looking over my shoulder.*

His good fortune was short lived and one of them was back hovering. He could feel them over his shoulder.

"What do you want?" he asked.

No answer, but he heard unusually heavy breathing.

"My God, Lisa! You brought your inhaler, didn't you?"

He turned to see if she were okay. It wasn't her.

What stood where he thought his sister would be, was a monster, the likes of which he had never seen before.

And he would never get to see again.

Toby couldn't wait to catch up with Lisa, James and Tonya. He had to pull a shift last night at the envelope company where he worked.

He was in charge of maintenance on the envelope lines. They broke down constantly. The owners were too cheap to buy new replacement parts and made most of their purchases on the used, secondary market.

Several envelope companies had gone out of business in recent years. Parts were currently available, but that market would dry up in a few short years. For him, it meant job security. But it also meant his time wasn't his own when they had a large order, like these first two days of his scheduled vacation.

A huge order came in with a tight deadline, and the owners apologized, but they needed him. The nice part was, as cheap as they were, they offered him double-time for the inconvenience. He couldn't turn that down.

He just turned off the blacktop. Their preferred campsite was a place they found all on their own. They had camped there several times. It was secluded, yet not horribly far from the lake.

In five minutes of slowly traversing the pitted dirt road, he would see their tent. He would be in time for lunch. Unfortunately, he had already missed one of James' famous bacon heavy breakfasts, which he loved.

A few minutes passed and he slowed his car, almost to a stop. The tent was collapsed. The fire was smoking out of control. Where were they?

He stopped and turned the car off. Something warned him to pull the pistol out of his glove compartment. He popped the full magazine into the weapon.

He exited the car slowly. Alarms were going off in his head. Lisa should have been running to him for an embrace. She was nowhere to be seen.

He slowly moved forward.

Chapter 14

The Second Incident

"Please sir, calm down. What has happened?" Milt asked, regretting being the one to answer the phone.

A young man was on the phone and trying to explain his emergency while fighting hysterics. Milt finally understood most of what he was saying. The young man had the presence of mind to read the GPS coordinates from his phone.

Milt turned to Steve and relayed the situation. Both Tom's were on duty and were given the coordinates. Milt and Steven jumped into Steve's SUV and headed that way as well.

Droves of people were coming out to the lake and surrounding forest. Here it was, Friday, and all hell was breaking loose. Steve was still reeling from his earlier phone conversation concerning Pinkerton's death and the missing remains.

He had shared the information with Milt. His men were law enforcement professionals as well, and they needed to know. He hadn't yet told the Toms about Tyke's remains being stolen, but he would.

But first, it sounded like a new crisis had presented itself.

Kong was full once again. In his short existence, he had never eaten so well. He was only a little over one year old, but because of the copious amount of growth hormones that he had been given, he was the size of an almost full-grown sasquatch. Physiologically, that would make him around six years old.

But intellectually and emotionally, he was a mess. The aggression training had made him into something quite different than any sasquatch before him.

Sasquatches, in general, were not man eaters. There had been, however, occasional incidents throughout their history alongside mankind where circumstances had allowed that to occur.

Kong was a new creation, emotionally and developmentally, because of man's interference. With him, there was no normal, usual or expected behavior.

He did not hide from men, but searched them out as a food source. Kong also confronted men because he saw them as weak and not worthy to share the same territory with him. He hated them. His inclination would always be to snuff them out, without reservation.

He was the monster that everyone feared would someday become a reality. Horror movies and literature had always used that premise to prey on man's fear. But that aggressive archetype never actually existed. No Frankenstein, Dracula or werewolf actually existed.

Kong does.

The young man ran to their vehicle. He was white as a sheet and his mouth was running a mile a minute. He was also holding a pistol.

Milt and Steve were the first to arrive. They immediately jumped out of the SUV and drew their weapons. They disarmed Toby.

He screamed, "I'm not the problem! Why are you taking my pistol? Something killed all my friends! Go look and do something about it!"

They tried to calm him down. He wasn't having any of it. They understood, but could do nothing while he ranted like a wild man.

The Toms pulled in, one after another. Bollman arrived first and then Deering. They got out and saw what was happening.

Ranger Bollman was the best at calming people down. It probably stemmed from his confidence to be able to handle himself physically in any situation. The team always went with each ranger's strengths.

Leaving Toby with Bollman, the other three rangers moved forward to discover what had happened.

The collapsed tent was immediately obvious. The fire was still smoldering. An Igloo ice chest laid on its side and broken eggs were strewn about.

A man, that Toby had called James, lay behind the tent. The two women were found farther into the woods. They had not been bitten in any way. It appeared that both had been bashed against the surrounding trees. Their injuries and blood spatter told that story.

James had been treated like Tyke. His face had been mostly chewed away. The balance of his physical being had also been dined upon at various locations. One arm had been completely removed and lay nearby.

This was no bear, mountain lion or pack of animals. This was something new. Steve already knew what that was.

He told his men what his thoughts were. They agreed.

Tom Deering unbuttoned his right uniform shirt pocket and pulled out a Polaroid, "I believe this is the beast we are looking for. It's hard to believe he can do this with only one hand, but I'm afraid it's true."

Tom was wrong, but it was a fairly logical conclusion. Until Kong's escape, Daryl was the only sasquatch in the region. Now the poor, one-handed beast was being blamed for Kong's misdeeds.

Kong picked up on the scent that had previously drawn him in this direction. It was getting stronger and more disconcerting. His primitive mind had no idea why.

It was familiar in some way. It also felt threatening. It wasn't one of the weak ones, but rather a creature like himself. It reminded him of the creature at the facility that he tried to attack. (He was remembering the day he tried to attack Clone B.)

The sooner he found the creature, the better. His limited reasoning was telling him that there was only room for one of them in this region, whatever the creature turned out to be.

It was too early for Daryl to show up. He spent his days doing who knows what. Gladys still decided to sit out on the porch and continue to crochet an afghan while she rocked the day away.

She had already set out some beef to thaw. Daryl was now finding his own food more often. Her beef bill was falling off, little by little.

She never minded feeding him. Her favorite thing to give him was sweets. His pleasured reactions were a boon to her soul.

She saw a movement at the tree line. That meant one of two things. Either deer were coming down for the field corn that she had set out, or Daryl was back.

She felt bad about the deer. She only started feeding them early on, when she realized Daryl could use some help finding his own food. It was a trap of sorts.

Daryl had picked off almost a dozen during his recovery. With his good hand, he could throw a rock with such accuracy that the poor creatures didn't stand a chance.

One throw would break a foreleg, and the poor, cute creatures would fall forward. Then he would pounce upon them. It was rather grotesque to watch, yet fascinating as well.

She had almost lost her stomach contents one day when one of his rock throws was too high and crushed the poor deer's skull. It collapsed immediately. It was horrible to watch. Why that bothered her more than his other takedowns, she wasn't sure.

She squinted at the tree line. Sometimes the deer were very shy and skittish. But if a deer bravely stepped forward, then there were usually three to five more to follow.

She finally got a decent view of her visitor, "Oh, my. It's my boy. Daryl, honey, come to momma! Your beef is still on the frozen side, but I have two pies you might enjoy! Pies, Daryl! Pies!"

He stepped from the shadows.

Her smile faded. Something wasn't right, but she couldn't put her finger on it. And then she realized, he had two hands.

For the first time in a long while, her joy was replaced by confusion and then fear.

Chapter 15

Daryl

Daryl spent most of his day hunting for food, even though he knew Gladys would always have food for him. But he had a deep yearning to continue to be a hunter, a predator.

For Daryl, predation wasn't cruel or sinister. He needed to eat and some animals were very edible. Simple as that.

At first, having only one hand was a hindrance. He learned quickly, out of necessity, the art of subterfuge. He learned patience.

His favorite thing to do was lie in wait along a deer trail. When his prey got close enough, he grabbed it, twisted its head almost a full three hundred and sixty degrees and then dined upon the animal while its life's blood was still pumping.

Every now and again, he would take one down with a rock. It seemed to please Gladys. He didn't know why, but there was much about her he didn't understand.

Like now. He was wearing a long, flat thing around his neck. She had tied it on him and repeated the word, *scarf,* over and over. He wasn't sure what it was for, but every time he showed up, she would say something and the word he could pick out was, *scarf.* She seemed pleased, so he didn't pull it off, although sometimes it was a nuisance.

Today he was just gamboling around the forest. It was his carefree happy movement. It was his acknowledgement that life was good, even with only one hand.

He ran for a while, very quietly, considering his great bulk. He was breathing extra heavy because of his physical exertion.

Much like a human that would complete a run, he bent at the waist. Daryl took deep breaths of the fresh springtime air.

Suddenly, he stood erect. He picked up a scent. It was hauntingly familiar and terribly frightening. He knew bear smell. He ruled out big cat or canines of any sort.

It smelled slightly like his mate, whom he hadn't seen in three years, and yet it was more familiar. And then his primitive thought center put together a very rational description of the scent.

It smelled like himself, only a bit distant. Like himself, but with a hard edge to it. Like himself, but it was something to fear.

All of that was brewing in his large cranial space. It was really too much for him to make much sense. His thought processes were on overload.

Because he found it disturbing, he wanted to find comfort in Gladys' presence. He immediately headed to his friend's house.

When he was almost to the wood line, he picked up her very comforting scent. He walked a few more yards. He stopped and sniffed the air.

He smelled her, but he smelled too much of her. Something was very wrong.

Then the faint scent that was causing him such consternation mingled in. This was wrong. He knew Gladys was in trouble, and he broke into a run from the tree line and headed straight for her house.

He saw her rocking chair was out. He saw her crochet yarn and needles. He didn't know what they were called, but they spoke of her presence.

And then he saw her small, crumpled body by the back door. He bounded past her rocker in the back yard and bounded onto the concrete stoop where she lay.

He knew death, but now he was learning grief.

With his one giant mitt, he gently stroked her head, which was turned at an odd angle. He was aware that this was her lifeless body.

And the disturbing smell that had upset him was surrounding her and mixing with her beautiful scent. The kind creature that he had learned to love, and that loved him was no more.

Whatever it was that smelled that bad had killed her. And he wanted to kill it. He would hunt it down.

His grief was mixing with rage. He sniffed the air to determine the escape route of the killer. He turned.

The killer stood at the tree line, downwind from Daryl. It had watched everything that transpired.

Daryl's first inclination was that he was looking at a distant reflection of himself. But even with his limited thinking, that didn't make sense.

He came down off the stoop and took several steps towards the interloper. It didn't move, but instead howled a warning.

Daryl reached for the wrought iron shepherd's hook, which held two of Gladys' favorite geranium baskets. He ripped it from the ground with his one good hand. The baskets of flowers went flying.

Daryl raised the wrought iron weapon into the air and snarled and then howled back at the intruder. The two beast's eyes locked.

This was a showdown, the likes that had never been witnessed in nature before. And truth be told, there were no witnesses to this event, except birds, squirrels and bunnies. And they were already scrambling for cover.

Kong trotted towards Daryl, and he in return worked at closing the gap between them. As they were almost on top of each other, Daryl swung the shepherd's hook.

It glanced off Kong's shoulder and traveled upward, opening a wound on the horrible beast's forehead. A roar of pain escaped his mouth, but this pain was nothing compared to the shock collar.

Kong had been surprised and never landed a blow. He felt his forehead, and then he looked at the blood on his hand.

A primal rage enveloped him and he sprang at Daryl. Daryl tried to get a second blow against the younger, larger beast. It didn't work.

Kong tore the shepherd's hook out his hands and threw it away. The monster re-engaged his grieving, one-handed opponent.

They grappled and rolled on the ground. Missing a hand was a distinct disadvantage. Daryl bit the enemy's forearm and Kong in turn bit his cheek and left a gaping hole on the left side of Daryl's face.

Daryl, as mad as he was about Gladys' death, just could not sustain the aggression level. Kong had the training, the experience to withstand pain and an unnatural supplanted aggression level.

But it was how the combat ended that was the most poignant. As they fought, Daryl's scarf flapped around his neck. It drew Kong's attention, and eventually he grabbed it.

Using it as a garrote, he held on to both ends, one in each hand. Pulling it as tightly as he possibly could, Kong strangled Daryl until he was dead.

After his foe was limp and lifeless, Kong had not yet worked through his rage. He spotted the discarded shepherd's hook, retrieved it and impaled the corpse of Daryl. In effect, he pinned him to the ground.

He then sat on his haunches, looking at the dead sasquatch. He felt that there was a connection with the dead beast. He then realized that he had, in a way, just killed himself.

Clone C smelled the thawing beef in Gladys' garage. An easy meal was just what he needed. The battle had left him totally spent, physically and emotionally.

Chapter 16

The Aftermath

In light of Pinkerton's murder and the stolen remains of Tyke Gillespie, Steve asked his guys what they thought they should do, regarding the new remains.

"Boss, if it does have something to do with that secret facility buried in Rothrock, then they'll get to whomever we give the bodies to. I mean, we're talking the U.S. government. They get what they want, no matter what," Tom Deering stated.

"Don't the state police have their own medical examiner?" Tom Bollman asked.

"No," Steve answered, "the coroner system is county based. The only other thing I can think to do is talk to the Pennsylvania Attorney General."

Milt asked a pertinent question, "Why does it even matter anymore? We know it's a sasquatch. It doesn't matter where it came from. Trying to expose the secret facility is a totally uphill battle. We need to kill a one-handed squatch."

"Squatch? You starting a new lingo?" Steve asked, smiling at Milt.

"If we are the first to publicly claim to be fighting a sasquatch, we should be the ones to come up with any cute Bigfoot talk," Milt declared.

"So what do we do, Steve? These bodies aren't getting any fresher," Bollman asked.

Toby had been interviewed and released. He had told them the name of a funeral home in Lewistown so his friends could be taken there.

"Tom, call that funeral home in Lewistown. We'll bag the girls and release them to the home. James has to be examined. We will need some kind of science supporting us or people will think we're crazy. They may anyway," Steve summarized.

"We still don't know what to do with James," Deering said.

"Nope. Not going to break protocol. Call the county ME. Pinkerton is dead, but Art Shuster, the Assistant ME, is still alive and kicking. If the same people steal another set of remains, we will have that as proof there is a conspiracy. But we will try to operate under the radar," Steve decided.

He called the county Medical Examiner's Office. The state police did not answer the phone. That was a good sign. He asked to talk to Shuster. Art came on the line.

Steve offered his condolences to Shuster, and then asked if he could slip out secretly and come to the ranger's station.

Art was more than intrigued. Steve promised him he would find the secrecy worthwhile. Art knew Steve and decided to trust him.

Once they had ended their call, Shuster waited an hour and then excused himself from his place of employment. Others thought he was upset over Doctor Pinkerton's murder, so they didn't press him on his need to leave the office.

Thirty minutes later, he was in Steve's office.

The hearse from a Lewistown funeral home was outside when he arrived. Three sets of remains, in three separate body bags, were lined up on the porch.

Art's first comment was rather humorous, "Um, Steve, don't you think having body bags on the front porch might be a little off putting for the tourists stopping by for information?"

Even under these circumstances, Steve couldn't help but laugh. He gave it right back to Art by saying, "It's part of a new public service campaign promoting safety in the woods. It's very effective."

Now Art was laughing.

"So why all the secrecy?"

Steve told him about the sasquatch hand and Angela Summers' death and then made the comparison to Doctor Pinkerton's death and Tyke Gillespie's missing remains. Then he explained the source of the new remains.

When he was finished, he looked at Art Shuster and waited for a reaction. Steve could see the gears turning.

Finally, Art asked, "So, if I accept the remains of this James fella, I could end up dead, at the hands of my own government?"

Steve thought to himself, *Shit. That didn't go well.*

He spoke up, "That's why I asked you here secretly. We are keeping a lid on this so no one knows. And don't work at night by yourself. Then the worst thing that could happen is a break-in and the stealing of the remains. You'll be safe."

"But once I do the autopsy, and let's say I insist a huge forest monkey killed him, then I may be a target. Right?" Art asked.

Steve sighed, "Art, me and my guys did our jobs. I tried to help you do your job safely. It's the best I can do. So are you going to do your job?"

"Well, today is your lucky day. I drove my minivan over here. Tell your guys to load him up."

The day ended with all bases covered. Steve and his men were exhausted. Unfortunately, some of their regular duties were getting neglected.

Tomorrow they would work at catching up.

Tom Deering stared at the Polaroid. He was sincerely worried about Gladys. The thing had been in her back yard.

His wife, Linda, asked what he was doing. He showed her the picture for the first time.

"Oh, Tom. Is that for real? It's huge! Are you safe out there?" It was the first time she had showed concern for him in a long time.

"Yes, dear. Me and the guys carry guns for that exact reason. We prefer being safe. Please, don't worry. You'll be packing my lunch for years to come."

"Why don't you leave your gun at home tomorrow," she joked.

"You're a riot, dear. Very funny. You should get a job as a comedian." He loved her sense of humor. It was one of the reasons he married her. She hadn't displayed that humor for a while. It felt good.

First thing in the morning, he would go check on Gladys. He needed to know she was safe.

And he hadn't had good chocolate chip cookies for a while.

Kong found a small cave to spend the night. His head hurt where Daryl had hit him with the shepherd's hook.

His nerves were still thrumming from the encounter with the other. The *other* was the easiest term he could find for a creature like himself. He remembered the *other* back at the secret facility.

He wasn't the only one of his kind. That did more to upset him than not. He had never been exposed to socialization.

Every aspect of his training and captivity worked towards making him narcissistic in every way. He was all that mattered.

He lay in his shallow cave trying to rest. He heard the howl of one of Pennsylvania's transplanted coyotes. Shortly after that, a hoot owl began its rhythmic chant.

Surrounded by life, he lay wishing he could destroy it all. Clone C was broken in every way. If he wasn't such a hateful and murderous creature, one could feel sorry for what the facility had done to him.

He hopped up quickly and exited the cave. He picked up a rock. He stood stock still and listened.

After a few minutes, he set his feet to balance himself and reared back and let the rock fly.

He heard a squawk, a quiet thud and pictured feathers floating gently to the ground. He had just killed the annoying owl.

He climbed back into the small cave and fell asleep. It would be a fitful sleep. Anything possessing that much hatred would never find peace.

Chapter 17

Finding Gladys and Daryl

Ranger Tom Deering stuck to his plan. Checking on Gladys Bomberger was a priority.

Pulling into her driveway, all appeared normal. She usually could hear his car tires on the gravel and would come out and greet him from the front porch.

He got out of the car and waited. Tom said a quick prayer. He wanted to see her on that front porch. She didn't show. He walked up her sidewalk and onto the porch and knocked.

No answer.

He then walked around the side of the house and headed to the garage to make sure her car was there. The side door of the garage was standing wide open.

As he entered, he smelled blood and meat. The big chest-freezer along the east wall had its lid open. Meat was strewn about, some of it still partially wrapped.

Her car was there. The entire scene made his heart sink. And then he saw a bit of matted hair hanging from a garden rake that was hanging on the wall near the freezer.

It wasn't Gladys' hair. He picked it off the rake and sniffed it. It smelled horrible. They always said the things were supposed to stink to high heaven and that sample sure qualified.

He pulled his pistol and slowly left the garage. This was all so wrong. He got on his radio, "Steve, I'm at Gladys Bomberger's house. Something is wrong here. Could you send me back-up? Over."

"Tommy B and Milt are tied up with a disturbance at the beach area. I'll come myself. I'm on my way. Sit tight. Over."

Steve ran out the door, locked it and hopped into his SUV. He put his emergency lights on as he drove. He didn't want Tom to be alone. The forest was becoming too dangerous. If his ranger thought something was wrong, then it was.

Tom moved slowly from the garage and continued around to the back of the house.

His heart sank for the second time when he saw her tiny body lying on the back stoop. He ran the rest of the way to get to her, but he already knew there was no hurry.

She was banged up rather badly, but not savaged like the men had been. *Thank God for small favors*, he thought.

He looked around while removing his pistol from his holster again. If it was here, he'd love to put a bullet in its head.

Past the shed, that had been featured in the Polaroid, and between the edge of her property line and the tree line, there was something huge lying in the grass. It had a stick or a pole of some sort sticking out of it.

He approached cautiously. Whatever it was, it didn't move. As he closed in, he could see it had hair all over its body. It had to be the squatch, he thought, borrowing Milt's term.

Now he was up on it. It was Glady's squatch, because it only had one hand. Someone, or something, had sunk Gladys' shepherd's hook through it, nailing it to the ground.

He remembered that she was so proud of the geraniums she had hung from it. The hook was heavy because it was made of wrought iron. To do this, it would have taken tremendous strength, super human strength. Or maybe, just sasquatch strength.

Steve was running across her backyard towards him.

Tom looked at his boss. He couldn't believe he was about to say his next words, "Steve, there are two."

Steve didn't comprehend the reference, "Two what? Two dead? Yes, I know. I saw Gladys on the way out here. Sorry, Tom. I know you liked her."

"Not what I mean, boss. There are two sasquatches. Well, this one is dead, but there were two."

Steve looked at the dead beast at their feet, "You know, Tom, using my Holmesian deductive skills, old one-hand, here, didn't die by the garden variety shepherd's hook. Look at his neck. His scarf is pulled as tight as one could get it without popping his head off. Notice the petechial hemorrhaging and the burst vessels in the eyes."

"Why the hell was he wearing one of Gladys' scarves?"

"We have a bigger problem. We now have an entire…" he paused and shook his head, "hand notwithstanding, an entire specimen of a sasquatch. If the secret lab was willing to kill for a hand and cover up evidence from victims, imagine what they would do to get this guy. I shudder to think," Steve intoned.

"There's a big chest freezer in the garage. Let's put him in there until we figure out what to do," Tom suggested.

Steve eyed the hairy corpse, "Is it big enough?"

"It's huge. It's an old GE 21.7 cubic foot. It'll hold him," Tom assured him.

"How do you know exactly what it is and the capacity? That's creepy."

"No. I was just in the garage. The thing is old, but like new. It still had the logo and capacity right on the front of it. I thought it was odd that a little old lady would have such a large freezer, but I figure Mr. Bomberger must have been a deer hunter," Tom explained.

"That's still huge for a deer hunter," Steve pointed out.

"Okay, listen. One day Gladys intimated that Mr. Bomberger would lure deer in with corn and do a little poaching. So that kind of explains the big freezer."

"Okay, how do we move him?"

"Rope and four-wheel drive. We'll drag him as close as possible and then figure it out from there."

They agreed. Thirty minutes later, the huge, dead carcass was lying in front of the open garage door.

They each grabbed an arm and tried pulling him across the smooth, concrete of the garage floor. The two men moved the corpse eight inches. They really weren't sure if they moved it or just stretched it.

Steve radioed Milt, "Are you guys done at the beach yet? Over."

"10-4. State police just hauled away three loud, obnoxious drunks. Everybody at the beach erupted in applause when they took them away. Over."

"You and Tom head to Gladys Bomberger's house, right now. Over."

"Be there in twenty. Over."

Steve took the time to address their next problem, "So it looks like one sasquatch killed the other sasquatch. Why?"

"Can we move Gladys inside and then talk?" Tom asked.

Steve was a bit embarrassed at his own insensitivity.

They carried the old women into what she called the parlor and laid her on the sofa. Tom covered her with one of her favorite afghans.

"Let's talk in the kitchen," Tom suggested.

Deering immediately began snooping and found the cookie jar. In it were his favorite cookies. He grabbed a plate and laid a dozen cookies on it.

"You want some milk?" he asked Steve.

Steve was just watching, somewhat amused.

Tom saw his expression, "She would want this. This is how she and I bonded all the time. You should have some cookies while we talk, to honor her memory."

Steve was ready to sit down and join in, but stopped to stare at the refrigerator door that Tom had just opened and closed while retrieving the milk.

"Stop feeding your face for a second and look at these Polaroids."

Tom joined him at the fridge door.

There was picture after picture of Daryl. He was wearing different scarves in some of them. In one, he was eating a deer alongside the shed. In another, he wore Gladys' wide-brimmed sun hat. In yet another, he was sitting on the stoop eating pie.

"You've got to be kidding me!" Tom said. "She hardly ever gave me pie."

Even in light of their circumstances, Steve started laughing. Tom had that ability.

"So the dead squatch was her pet. So going by that narrative, the bad squatch killed her, and the good squatch got killed trying to save her. Or something like that," Tom surmised. "How's that for Holmesian skills?"

"Not bad, Watson. Now gather those photos. That's more evidence of the thing's existence."

They sat back down and ate their cookies and milk while waiting for Tom B and Milt.

Chapter 18

Two Dilemmas

The four men were exhausted. Getting Daryl into the freezer was an arduous task. But there was good news: he fit.

This left them with two, yet unsolved, problems. The first was, to whom do they report the discovery of the century? They had an actual, intact sasquatch (minus a hand).

The second dilemma may be a little more daunting. How would they find an angry, murderous monster before someone else was killed? And problem two (part B), what would it take to kill it?

They realized while getting the muscular, heavy monster into the freezer, that a conventional 9mm round from one of their service pistols may be terribly inadequate to bring down a raging seven or eight-hundred-pound beast.

They had already seen its handiwork. A human was not even a hindrance to the thing, so they resolved to carry 12-gauge shotguns while on duty.

Steve ordered four locking mounts, one for each of their cars. They could then carry the powerful weapon upright on the passenger side.

A state motor pool guy from Harrisburg was scheduled to stop by tomorrow to install them. This particular day was about shot.

"So, how do we lure it out, Steve?" Milt asked.

The Toms were all ears. They hadn't a clue what to do next.

"Look at all this beef we have thawing here. Maybe that will be enough. Grab that empty plastic garbage can in the corner."

Tom B grabbed it, and they began to unwrap and load the previously frozen beef into the garbage can. There was almost two hundred pounds of beef.

The plan was to return to Gladys' house tomorrow with shotguns, use the beef as bait and wait. With any luck, the thing would show up, they'd shoot it and call it a day.

It was by no means a perfect plan, but they had yet to see what they were up against. The dead sasquatch was frightening enough. They couldn't imagine seeing one in action.

A horn blew and got their attention. A hearse from the local funeral home had come to pick up Gladys' remains. Steve hadn't decided to what he was going to attribute her death.

The two-man mortuary crew looked at the old woman and how banged up she was. They then looked at Steve.

"She fell down the cellar steps. Pretty bad tumble."

The one guy shrugged and mumbled, "Too bad."

The second man on the team said, "Holy shit, dude! How many times did she fall down them steps?"

They loaded her up and left.

"Cellar stairs? The poor woman looked like she had done ten rounds with Mike Tyson and then fell down the steps," Milt said, wondering how Steve was going to report this.

"Don't worry. My official report will be sasquatch attack, just like the others. If someone disputes it, we show them our frozen buddy."

"Let's go. Anybody up for a drink?" Steve asked.

All three asked when and where.

Steve answered, "Follow me home."

While driving home, he called Cindy and told her that the guys were coming. She offered to get the alcohol that they had on hand and set it up on the sideboard with a bucket of ice.

It was time for letting off a little steam.

The beast had watched the weak ones play on the lake. The things they moved on were fascinating. A few had gotten very close to shore.

He had searched his immediate area for good sized rocks to throw, but there were none. He wanted to hurt them and disrupt their play time.

How could there be so many? He was strong and the master of his domain wherever he went. It made no sense that the weak ones were so plentiful. They died so easily.

Tomorrow he would search for good throwing rocks. Their smiles and laughter would disappear. He would control the water and the land.

His thought patterns were not that far removed from some humans. Tomorrow would prove to be a pivotal moment for him and the weak ones.

Art Shuster had been the Assistant ME in Huntingdon county for seven years. He had served as an Assistant ME in Palm Beach County, Florida for three years.

As he examined the remains of young James, he checked off the possibilities as he eliminated them.

He talked aloud into his recorder, "Not a big cat, not a bear, not a wolf or any other canine, not an alligator. What the hell does that leave me to blame? A human with a really big mouth."

Pause.

"The amount of strength needed for some of these injuries, is beyond a human's capabilities. The bite marks suggest a hominid. The only known hominid capable of this kind of damage is a gorilla. Plain and simple."

Pause.

"I use the phrase, *known hominid*, because it has been suggested that an unknown species is responsible for what I'm witnessing.

"My identification may be slightly antiquated, for some are currently classifying human like creatures as hominin instead of hominid."

Pause.

"There is no evidence here that allows me to claim the assailant was bipedal, although I can't imagine a four-legged creature pulling and tearing as is demonstrated by these injuries."

Pause.

"I quipped about a human with a big mouth. The bite patterns suggest something human-like, but they appear three times larger than what an average human could hope to achieve."

Pause.

"I render that identification is inconclusive."

He reached up and turned the recorder off.

His lab assistant, Jill, asked, "What do you really think?"

He remembered the warning Steve had given him about the secret lab. Rather than place anyone in danger, he responded, "Inconclusive. I would rule out human and all of the animals that I named earlier. After that, your guess is as good as mine.

"Place him in a drawer, and call his family to find out where to direct the remains."

He pulled his gloves off and threw them away. Art headed to his office and picked up the phone.

Cindy came into where the guys were unwinding, "Honey, Art Shuster is on the line." She handed him the wireless handset.

He went into the next room. When he came back, the guys were quiet.

"Well, what did Shuster say?" Tom B asked.

"He's meeting me at Gladys' house in the morning. I'm going to show him the sasquatch."

"Why?" Milt asked.

"He needs a bite impression to confirm what killed James. He's pretty much convinced it's a new creature. I want to give him the proof he needs to call a spade a spade."

Chapter 19

Bait

Steve was the first to arrive at Gladys' garage. A while later, Art arrived. Steve couldn't wait to see Art's reaction.

He showed Art into the garage. The man looked around and said, "Okay. Where's the patient?"

Steve lifted the lid on the freezer.

Art's eyes got as big as saucers. He leaned in closer and sniffed. "Phew! Even frozen, the thing stinks. You know, Steve, it's one thing to talk about it, but to see it in person. It's enormous! And if it wasn't bent in half like that, it would be even more impressive."

"Okay," Steve conceded, "let's sit him up."

Steve grabbed around the beast's shoulders and pulled back. The corpse was stiff, and it took quite a bit of effort, but Steve sat him up.

"What now, Art?"

"We need to open his mouth," Art told him.

Art held the sasquatch's forehead, and Steve pushed down on the chin. As the mouth opened, a pocket of gas escaped.

"Holy shit! That is the worst smell that ever violated my nose!" Steve declared.

Art laughed, "You don't work with dead people much, do you?"

"No. Thank God. What next?"

"I mix these two tubes together. The compound puffs up like foam. I shove it in his mouth. Shut his mouth. Then we pry it open again. I pull the compound out. It hardens. And, voila. I have a print of a sasquatch bite pattern."

Ten minutes later, Art was done.

"Does it look like anything?"

"Not yet. I'll go back and make a cast of this impression and test the similarities with the examination material."

"Art, you realize that we don't think this sasquatch did what you saw. There is a second one out there, and he's mean."

"I got it, Steve. But if it is the same species, the similarities should be evident. Give me a little time," Art told him and then asked, "What are you going to do with the body?"

"I don't know yet, but don't tell anyone," Steve insisted.

"Your secret is safe with me," the Assistant ME assured him.

Art pulled out as Milt and the Toms were arriving.

The rangers got right to work. The Toms each took a handle of the plastic trash can full of meat and walked past the shed.

About twenty yards from the shed, they emptied the can. They were hoping a big, smelly pile of meat would draw the sasquatch back to Gladys' house, if it was still in the area.

The thinking was that it was at the Bomberger's home once, why not again?

The rangers would wait, two inside the shed and two inside the kitchen at the back door.

They were in place and willing to wait all day.

The beast found what it imagined was a good spot to punish the weak. There were plenty of rocks and a clear view from the tree line.

The beast was excited. The thought of hurting and killing his enemy was filling him with joy.

The secret facility had created a psychopath.

It was early and not many of the weak had taken to the lake.

He would wait.

Three hours passed. It was almost noon. No sign of the beast. Steve, who was in the kitchen with Tom Deering, pulled his phone out of his pocket as it rang.

Caller ID showed it was Art Shuster, "Yeah, Art. What do you got?"

"It is an identical beast to the one you have on ice." Art confirmed.

Steve already knew what Art just confirmed, but they were building a scientific argument for the beast's existence in case something happened to their squatchcicle.

He still hadn't figured out to whom they would share the dead sasquatch's remains. If they had any luck, they would have two bodies to share with the world.

Tom Deering was shameless. He went through Gladys' freezer and found a gallon ice cream tub full of chocolate chip cookies.

"You know, I always wondered how she always had just baked a dozen cookies. She was pulling one over on me," Tom said, acting disappointed.

Steve shook his head, "Tom, they are still homemade. She just stocked up so she would never disappoint you when you dropped by. That's pretty sweet if you ask me."

"Crap! You're right. I'm going to miss her. Do you want a cookie?" he offered.

"No. These are the last she made. You enjoy them," Steve suggested.

They continued to wait for their trap to bear fruit.

The lake was getting crowded. Sailboats, sailboards, jet skis, motorboats and houseboats were everywhere. Canoers and kayakers were gliding all over as well.

Kong watched. Several of the weak were getting close to where he lay in wait.

Two young men in kayaks came floating along at the shoreline. Kong's pulse quickened and his breathing became heavier.

He saw his shot. He positioned himself and let the projectile fly. It hit one of the young men in the chin and neck.

The target dropped his paddle and raised his hands to his throat. He was gagging and gasping for breath. It happened so quickly that his friend didn't even realize his buddy was hurting.

Instead, he chided him for dropping his paddle.

"Hey, Justin. How in the hell did you lose your paddle?" The friend froze for a moment. He couldn't understand what Justin was doing. He appeared to be holding his face.

When Justin's hands dropped and slumped forward, he saw the blood. He immediately screamed to nearby boaters. Some were part of a group they were with.

"HELP! HELP! Something is wrong with Justin!"

Several people heard him and began heading towards the men.

A second rock flew and crashed into the bow of the friend's kayak, almost tipping it over. The man saw the rock hit and began frantically paddling away from his friend.

Another big rock splashed in the water to his left. Several who were making their way to help saw the missile flying and splashing into the lake.

Someone yelled, "Somebody's launching rocks from shore! Look!"

Another rock flew, hitting the second man in the back. It too hit hard enough that his paddle flew out of his hands.

A nearby boat cut its engine and drifted towards the kayaker to save him. Stunned by the blow to his back, he couldn't raise his right arm to help pull himself into the boat.

Justin, still slumped and apparently unconscious, drifted even closer to shore.

The target was too tempting, and Kong launched several more rocks at the lifeless looking man. They hit their mark, and the assembling witnesses were appalled.

One of the boaters had a pistol. There was absolutely no need for a pistol on this lake, but he thought it made him look cool. He never thought he'd actually use it.

As he got closer to shore, he saw where the rocks were coming from. He saw Justin get battered and feared he was most likely dead. He felt justified shooting in the direction of the rock launcher. So he did.

Kong saw where two of the bullets hit the trees. It was time for him to leave. His game was successful. He hoped to do it again.

He vacated his position. The sasquatch, after all the excitement, was hungry.

Steve's phone rang. It was Millie at the marina. He answered, "Brighton, what's up?"

"Where the hell are you guys? I bet your office phone and marine radio are burning up with calls!" she said, angrily.

"Calm down. What happened?"

"Steve, I heard over the radio, some guy was launching large rocks from the shore and killed a boy in a kayak and injured a second boy. And one of the rescuers has a gun and is shooting into the woods."

"Millie, I'll have someone there in a jiffy. Get on the radio and tell them to stop shooting a gun on the water. And call an ambulance for the boys."

He ended the call and burst out the back door and headed to the shed. He yanked the door of the small building open and hollered, "Milt! Tom! Get back to the marina! Code 3! Somebody launched rocks from the shoreline and killed a kayaker, injured a second one and some asshole is shooting into the woods. Get going! See Millie!"

Both men bolted to their cars, hopped in and tore out with red lights and siren blaring.

The rock launching was bad enough, but shooting across water was extremely dangerous. Most people don't realize that bullets can easily ricochet on water. Ricochets can go on for a great distance, much like skipping a stone.

Tom Deering and Steve were now left to mind the bait. And Tom had a good question, "Can sasquatches throw rocks?"

"I don't have a clue, but stupid people can. Or they can use one of the rubber launchers that they use at county fairs to launch pumpkins and other things that weren't meant to fly. That kind of device was the first thing I thought of when Millie used the term, *launch*. Hell, they might have killed a kid."

"If you want to head back, I can mind the meat," Tom offered.

"By yourself? I don't think so. If the thing shows up, I'm hoping the two of us are enough."

Chapter 20

Minding the Meat

Kong left the shoreline looking to find food. One of the weak ones would be just fine, but with all the commotion at the lake, it may prove difficult to find one alone or in a small group.

Then he smelled it, carried on a gentle breeze. It was the scent of slowly rotting meat. Although Kong was a hunter, he was just as much an opportunist. And he smelled what could be an easy meal.

During his aggression training, his captors would often feed him scraps of garbage, from their own dumpster at the facility. Rotting meat and vegetables was nothing new to him.

That part of the training was to condition him to all situations when fresh rations were not available. He needed to adapt or improvise to receive his daily caloric requirement.

Since leaving the facility, he had lost over fifty pounds. It made him leaner and faster. He felt fine without the extra weight. But right at this moment, he was famished.

The raw meat was beckoning. He hoped it was plentiful, like maybe an entire dead deer.

The General said to the assembled group, "We should have heard something by now. That monster should be killing people right and left. But since that one man's death at the lake, we have heard nothing. How do you explain that?"

Doctor Nolte raised his hand.

"Yes, Doctor. What have you to say on the matter?"

"Your men killed the medical examiner and stole a set of remains. Maybe someone was smart enough to put two and two together. They may be purposefully shielding their casualties to throw us off."

"I see, Doctor. And whom might you think would be that smart?"

"The rangers, General. They turned over the original hand that we have used for our clones. It then disappeared and the lab director was shot. That was followed some time later with someone being shot and more missing remains. If you'll excuse my scientific humor, it's not rocket science."

"And where do you think the victims are being held?" the General asked.

"Right under our noses, General. They are just attributing the deaths to something else. I would have your investigators look at deaths around the lake. That is where the first attack occurred, so start there."

"You may have something, Doctor. Good work."

The meeting ended on that note.

He stood over a pile of loose, trimmed, rotting meat. Kong was no dummy. Rather than dive into devouring this pile of good fortune, he remained upright and scanned his surroundings.

"My God, Steve! Look at him! Seeing a live one is more impressive than dealing with the dead one. He's sniffing the air instead of eating. He must be more intelligent than what we thought," Tom pointed out.

"Are you ready? We spring out of here and run right at him. And then we let our shotguns do the talking. On three. ONE! TWO! THREE!"

Tom B and Milt got to the marina. People were going crazy. Watercraft coming back to the marina in a hurry and others were rushing out to help.

Millie met them, and several others tried to engage them. It was a zoo. Tom listened to Millie as Milt fired up the ranger's tug boat.

The ambulance pulled in as Millie related everything she knew. He waved them over. No one had yet brought the injured boys back to the marina, but one boat had radioed that they had them.

The badly injured young man, Justin, was not dead, but he was in a bad way. Tom asked Millie to hail the boat and find out their ETA.

She did. They were just pulling into Slip 25. They directed the ambulance crew to that location. Milt kept the tug running, but disembarked to ask the new arrivals at Slip 25 the exact location where the incident occurred.

Tom told the group not to leave, while he and Milt headed to the scene. They agreed that some would stay and some would go with their injured friends.

Milt and Tom headed out to the eastern shore. They could see a group of boats still in the area and clearly, some of the men had off-loaded and were milling around on the shore looking for the offender.

"Crank it up, Milt! We need to preserve the scene and diffuse this situation. If they find the guy, they're going to kill him!"

Milt pushed the throttle forward. The tug was in very good condition, but was old. He needed to be careful not to overdo it.

Tom had donned the hip waders in preparation for going ashore. He then took over the wheel to allow Milt to do the same thing.

They were finally at the shore line, and Milt let the tug drift in. Once positioned, he dropped anchor to prevent her from drifting badly.

Both rangers jumped off to reclaim a semblance of order. To the six men walking along the shoreline, he asked, "Which one of you fired at the perpetrator?"

One guy answered, "None of us. Those guys took off as soon as they saw your tug coming. They knew not to have guns out here."

"Do you know who had the weapon?" Tom asked.

"No, sir. The lake is crowded with a lot of non-locals. I wish they'd stay the hell away," the guy stated.

Five mumbled agreements followed.

"Did any of you get a glimpse of the suspect?" Milt asked.

"Tell him, Randy," one of the bystanders said.

"Which one of you is Randy?" Milt asked.

A short, blonde haired man raised his hand, "I am."

Tom asked the pertinent question, "What would you like to tell us, Randy?"

"When the clown in the boat started shooting at the shore line, I saw something big move away from the area where the rocks were flying."

"Something?" Tom asked.

The short man answered, "I guess I mean someone. It was probably a trick of the light, but the guy was huge. Like, Ripley's Believe It Or Not kind of huge. Like I said, probably a trick of the lights."

"Where exactly did you see the guy?" Tom asked.

The short man pointed to a specific spot, "Between the two maples, where all the partridgeberries are growing."

"Thank you, fellas. My partner and I will take it from here." The men began heading back to their own watercraft.

The one whom had originally spoken up turned and said, "Watch out for the huge pile of shit back there. I think a bear must have been holding it in all winter."

"Thanks for the warning, buddy," Tom responded.

As soon as the men were out of range, Tom almost jumped out of his skin, "The guy said he was huge. And we have to find this big pile of shit. We may have found our sasquatch."

They did find the scat. It wasn't bear scat or any other animal excrement with which they were familiar. They also found a pile of five rocks

Each rock weighed about four to five pounds. They were heavier than a man could accurately throw for any distance. The real convincer were the strands of reddish-brown hair they discovered.

Tom B smelled the sample. Oh my God! It smells just like the one we dumped in the freezer. Maybe worse!"

"Worse?" Milt questioned. "I went home and showered for thirty minutes. My wife complained that my clothes smelled worse than the fertilizer she uses on the garden!"

"Smell it," Tom B challeneged.

Milt, being a man who couldn't walk away from a challenge, took a whiff. "Yes, that is squatch. And it beats the freezer boy we loaded. WOW!"

"What do you want to do now?" Tom B asked.

"We need to go interview those people, quickly. And then get back to Tom and Steve. Let's go!"

They climbed back on the tug and headed towards the marina.

Chapter 21

Shotguns

Bursting out through the shed door, the two lone men ran directly at their quarry. Both had already jacked a round into the chamber.

The monster stood, unmoved, either in surprise or defiance. They were not sure which. As they quickly closed the distance between them, it snarled and then howled.

As they advanced, it almost welcomed the challenge. It broke towards them at the last second. They were not expecting that. Tom stopped, aimed and fired.

The beast howled in pain and halted.

Steve replicated Tom's actions, only he was closer. The monster seemed to swat the air as if bees were attacking. Both men fired again.

It stooped, picked up a field stone and flung it at Steve. He tried to duck, but not as effectively as he could have done. It hit him, first his shotgun and then his left shoulder.

He went down without a sound, and Tom fired a third time. They were all fifty feet apart, in a triangular formation.

The beast, thinking Steve was down for the count, charged at Tom. Its speed did not correlate with its size. It was freaky fast.

Tom discharged his weapon one more time, blowing a chunk of matted fur off its shoulder. It reached him and grabbed the shotgun, ripping it from his grip and breaking three fingers in the process.

It threw the weapon thirty feet from where they stood. It was about to make its final move to obliterate Tom's existence.

Steve was right behind it and leveled his shotgun at its left leg, from only a few feet away. The leg splintered as fur, muscle and blood sprayed the field. Lacking that support, the creature toppled on its side.

Before it could recover, Steve stepped in and discharged a round at its head. The top of its skull gave way and the gray matter contained therein spilled out onto the ground.

Its chest was moving back and forth like a bellows. One eye seemed to be focused on Steve. The other was covered in gore.

Tom had gone to retrieve his own gun. His broken hand prevented him from delivering the death blow with his recovered shotgun.

This is the beast that killed Gladys, so Tom should have the pleasure, Steve thought. He then racked his last round into the chamber.

Tom yelled, "KILL IT, STEVE!"

Steve handed him the primed weapon and said, "No, this is your baby."

Tom rested the weapon across his forearm, in the crook of his elbow, aimed at the monster's head and pulled the trigger.

The bellows ceased. An audible exhalation or sigh escaped Kong's lips. He was dead.

Tom looked to the sky, "There you go, Gladys."

The two men were both silent, processing what they had witnessed, what they had done and what needed to happen next.

Tom broke the silence, which was really no surprise, when comparing the two personalities.

"This one is bigger than the other. I don't think GE makes a freezer this size."

Steve began laughing. A reaction to Tom's comment, of course, but also as a release of fear and stress.

"Hey, I know a trucker who has a reefer. I could call him, and we could keep both animals cold. He also has a small forklift. It could work."

"Who do we tell?"

"No one," the General said.

Both men spun around to see almost a dozen men in military camouflage fatigues standing behind them. All were holding automatic weapons, at the ready.

"I'm General Wartman. The animal you just killed, congratulations, by the way, belonged to the United States government. He was a mean son of a bitch. I'm surprised you dispatched him so easily. He killed five of my guys before he escaped."

"What do you want?" Steve asked.

"Well, Ranger Brighton, I want my animal back. He's still valuable for research. And I want the one you have in the freezer in the garage. And lastly, I want your assured silence on the matter. This is all classified."

"What if I say no?" Brighton asked.

"Look, Angela Summers' death occurred because of an overzealous civilian contractor. He messed up, so we eliminated him from the payroll. Doctor Pinkerton tried to resist. He answered the door with a pistol in his hand. That type of resistance won't be tolerated against military troops. It was unfortunate."

"What's your point, Wartman?" Steve pushed.

"For us to maintain our secrecy, sometimes people die. But it doesn't have to be that way. Your buddy, Art Shuster, is completely onboard. Leaving a trail of dead bodies doesn't do anyone any good. But my main point is, a few more isn't going to make a big difference to us."

"So you are threatening us?" Tom asked.

He ignored Tom and continued the conversation with Steve, "You wouldn't want anything to happen to your rangers, just like I didn't want anything to happen to my men. And that Cindy of yours, what a cutie. A little snoopy for my tastes, though. Keep them all safe, Steve. Just walk away. A good day's work completed."

Steve was seething inside, but he knew when he was beat. They were outgunned, and the mention of Cindy and her ability to ferret out information brought him in line with the General's wishes.

"Let's go, Tom. Our work here is done."

Tom couldn't believe this situation, but he understood Steve's reaction. He had no choice.

Tom walked to his vehicle.

Steve radioed Tom B and Milt and told them that operations were done. And that they should stay near the office for a debriefing.

After they left, another dozen more soldiers descended on the Bomberger's property. They retrieved the corpses, washed and disinfected the freezer and even cleaned up the rotting meat. Anything that could be used as evidence was gone.

When Steve and Tom returned to the office, Steve began working on Tom's hand. He had quite a bit of advanced first aid training.

Tom B and Milt finished their interviews and couldn't wait to hear about how they had taken down the monster.

Rangers Brighton and Deering told them about the final battle. And then Steve took over to prepare them for the blow to come.

When he was finished, Tom Bollman stood up and yelled, "This is bullshit! They hold the only concrete proof of sasquatches' existence, and they are going to suppress it! Why would they do that?"

"I've been thinking about that. I think the monster we killed was a clone. Possibly grown, for a lack of a better term, from the hand that went missing. And it's the military. What does the military want more than anything?

"Tactical advantage in the field. An army of sasquatches, if at all possible, would give them that. And if sasquatches continue to not exist, then no other government will be looking for their own squatch or looking to steal ours."

"Sounds as plausible as any explanation," Milt agreed. "So, what are we going to do about it?"

"How does insurrection sound?" Steve asked.

He had their attention.

"That facility isn't that large. At best, the General commands maybe three dozen men. What if we flood the area with hunters? Throw them off their game," Steve suggested.

"Then what?" Milt asked. "So we have a bunch of hunters out there."

"What if they are all friends of Tyke Gillespie? What if they find out the truth and want a little payback? A hundred armed and pissed off men who can shoot a rifle better than they can drive a car. A grudge match to take down the facility."

"You know that General has to be watching us pretty closely to see if we stay quiet. How are we going to get the word out?" Tom B asked.

"For now, we don't. We play nice and stay out of trouble. But come November, during deer season, we will have the tactical advantage. What do you say?" he asked his men.

Tom D said, "I'm in."

"Me too," Tom B and Milt both confirmed.

"Now, fill me in on what lies I must come up with for today's calamities," Steve inquired.

Chapter 22

November

Steve and his men bided their time. The warm fall days, which some have deemed as Indian summer, were gone. Chilly days, which sometimes included flurries and light dustings of snow, had arrived. Steve never forgot what needed to be done.

It was only one day away from regular arms deer hunting season. In Pennsylvania, there was as much excitement and enthusiasm around this activity as there was for Thanksgiving and Christmas. Slight exaggeration only.

Steve and his men were more excited for this year's hunt than any year previously. This was their time to even the score against a small, tyrannical outpost in the Rothrock State Forest.

Tyke Gillespie was a legend while he was alive. Being deceased had elevated his status. Steve was going to address his hunting club.

He was to address them on hunter safety, as he did every year on the night before regular arms season began. This year would be different.

These talks usually had over a hundred hunters in attendance. Most were there because a brand new Remington Model 7600 was being raffled, and it was their annual bean soup dinner.

Steve started rather differently than usual. He had brought his laptop and projector. As the men sat waiting for him to begin, he walked on stage.

The room quieted down a little. But many of the men continued to talk, sharing family updates, talking about their rifles and telling crude jokes. Even though they were inside a building, over half of them were still wearing their hunting caps.

Steve projected an image of Tyke Gillespie on the screen. His date of birth and his date of death were displayed across the bottom.

As soon as it appeared, the men stopped talking. The room not only became silent, almost every participant in tonight's affair had removed his hat. *That*, Steve thought, *is great respect.*

"How many of you remember this man?" he began.

Every hand was raised.

"How many of you know me?" Again, almost every hand was up.

"How many of you trust me?" About the same number of hands were raised again.

"My rangers and I know what killed Tyke. And I'm going to tell you a story. A true story. When I am finished, some of you are going to be doubters. But this is no joke, and we need your help."

The tale he wove included everything and everybody. His rangers joined him on stage to show their solidarity with their boss. Heads were nodding, some head were getting scratched, but they all listened to the end.

"Here's where the rubber meets the road. On Monday, tomorrow, forget your first day of deer season. We need you to help us take down the secret facility in Rothrock.

"With all of us hunters looking to even the score for Tyke's death, they can't win! We will outgun them and close them down!"

This was the moment of truth, "Who's with us?"

The men stood and the room erupted. He had his answer. Tomorrow was D-Day in the forest.

He worked at getting the room quiet once again.

"Listen to what I am about to say very carefully. This must remain a secret until its over. If just one person leaks this, we could be sunk. With over one hundred men here, the odds are against it remaining a secret. I am counting on your honor, and then I am counting on your rifle."

Heads nodded. They at least looked like they were onboard.

"FOR TYKE!" Steve shouted and the room erupted.

He had given them the instructions during his speech about the time and the place to meet. Steve didn't feel great about moving forward, but he had no other plan.

He and his rangers had recruited several others. What they really had going for them was the current and terrible mistrust of the government.

It was now just a countdown. The rangers had sent their wives, girlfriends and loved ones on a retreat to a camp near Pittsburgh. If things went wrong, they weren't sure how vindictive the General would be.

The General had a few of his resources watching the rangers for almost seven months. They seemed to be totally controlled by his not so veiled threats.

He stopped having them watched three weeks ago. They would be overwhelmed by their duties during deer season, he reasoned. He needn't worry about them. All was going as planned.

Three new clones were developing. They were in the toddler stage. There were no more isolated clones or pets. He was having the scientists mix following commands with aggression training, like one would use with a police dog.

It was very early, but there were signs of success.

To make the facility more focused, he had destroyed all the other projects except the badgers. They had changed the badger compound. It now had a metal bottom and metal sides, so they could no longer tunnel out.

They hadn't yet perfected them to take orders, but the General loved their increased size and aggressive behavior.

Monday morning at 6:00 a.m., the hunters began showing up at the staging area on Route 26. Everyone was supposed to be there by 6:30 a.m. and ready to go.

By the appointed time, ninety-one hunters from Tyke's club were ready to board the busses. It was better than Steve had hoped.

Adding another twenty-two men, which included Steve and his rangers and their friends, they had enough to accomplish the mission. They boarded the vehicles that would transport them towards their target.

By 7:10 a.m. they were ready to leave the vehicles behind and go the rest of the way on foot. Today would make history. Steve hoped they would be on the right side of that history.

They needed to cover two miles through the forest. Steve divided his forces into two groups. One group was led by himself and Ranger Deering, and the other half of the men was led by Rangers Bollman and Cox.

There was a natural split about three quarters of a mile from the secret compound. That is where the forces would separate into two groups.

The morning passed slowly as they trudged along in the two inches of snow that had fallen overnight. They were observing radio silence. Once into position, they were to send a series of three clicks, several times.

The time came where the clicks were communicating the readiness of the groups to move in. The mission was beginning as fences were being cut.

The General sat in his office going through a huge list of emails. He was regularly falling behind in clearing up his electronic communication.

He was old fashioned. He liked using the telephone. It was instantaneous and very rarely were phrases and comments misunderstood. You could almost always discern the other person's mood.

Emails were too ambiguous for conversation. Relaying facts and figures were fine. He deleted one after another, from persons with whom he wished not to communicate.

What is this? he thought. An email from a local acquaintance from years ago. He opened it and read every word twice. His face turned red as he filled with rage.

He yelled for his assistant.

Captain Tomsick entered his office, "Yessir."

"Sound the damn alarm! We're under attack! Get everyone ready to repel the enemy!" the General ordered.

Tomsick hesitated, the old man sounded like he had finally lost his mind. The captain had seen this day coming.

"Damn it, Tomsick! Carry out my orders!"

The captain asked the General, "Sir, what makes you think we are under attack?"

"I just received an email from an old friend. The rangers are mounting an offensive. Now, do as you're told, or I will bust you down to second lieutenant!"

Tomsick left his office to follow the orders and sound the alarm. He hit the red button mounted on the wall behind his desk. Usually, it was sounded when an experiment had gotten loose. The squad would be unprepared for this, if it was real.

The troops were assembled in their staging area, expecting another young sasquatch hunt or a more dangerous badger hunt. Everything else had been destroyed.

The General strode into the room. Someone yelled, "ATTENTION!"

"At ease, damn it! Men, we are under attack! Secure our perimeters! The rangers from Raystown Lake are mounting an assault!" He realized how silly that sounded, but he knew it could be true. His threats could have easily pissed them off.

His men moved out to secure their fence line. The General wished they were on a much larger piece of property.

As soon as soldiers appeared, the hunters found cover and aimed their weapons. Steve saw them resting their weapons on stumps, logs and against tree trunks.

The scene reminded him of what he had read about the Minutemen of the American Revolution. It was a far more romantic notion than what the situation warranted, but he thought it anyway.

The soldiers had not seen them yet. On his bus, he had instructed the hunters to not shoot until told, or until it was absolutely necessary. He truly thought there was a chance to do this at a minimum cost of life.

A group of seven soldiers walked into their kill zone. Steve stood and held his hands up.

"STOP! Gentlemen, right now, there are a hundred rifles trained on you. Marksmen of the highest caliber. Lay down your weapons."

The soldiers immediately crouched down in defensive positions. This was obviously a seasoned team.

Their leader, whose rank was indeterminate, asked "How do we know you're not bluffing?"

Steve had two snipers on his team. They were friends whom had served in Afghanistan. Two better shots could not be found.

Steve called out, "Donnie! Aaron! Show the man!"

Two shots cracked the crisp air almost simultaneously.

The lead soldier's weapon flew out of his hands, as did the man's behind him. Both men jumped back in fear, realizing that their life or death was at someone else's whim. They rubbed their hands and forearms which still felt the sting of the weapon's violent exit from their grips.

The leader issued the command, "Men! Drop your weapons!"

The men stood and threw their weapons down.

Milt and four of the hunters rushed forward to gather them up and check for handguns, which they found. Milt applied zip ties around the wrists of the prisoners and marched them back behind their lines.

Steve gave the signal to move forward. The prisoners watched in awe as over sixty men came out of hiding and advanced towards the compound.

A second group, of about eleven soldiers, had set up behind barricades closer to the buildings.

"This is Captain Tomsick," came a voice from behind the barricades. "You are trespassing on government property! Turn around and leave or risk facing deadly force to halt your approach!"

Steve and the advancing hunters stopped. He yelled, "SCATTER!"

The hunters dropped to the ground behind whatever cover they could find. Steve ducked behind a tree.

"Captain Tomsick, this is Ranger Steve Brighton! This is a no-win situation for you! Give up, before American soldiers and American citizens get injured! We are not leaving until this facility is shut down!"

Tomsick responded, "Why do you want this facility closed? It is involved in research to help America win wars against our enemies, both foreign and domestic."

Steve almost laughed. Tomsick sounded like a propaganda film. Steve answered, "It's that domestic part that your General is screwing up. He is targeting innocent citizens! One man who was killed was a friend of all these men aiming rifles at you. He was killed by your rabid sasquatch! This has to stop!"

Tomsick knew the General's heavy-handed dealings with innocent people was going to bite them on the ass one day. The old man, at times, acted like he was a mafia kingpin instead of a United States military man. Unfortunately, Tomsick and his men couldn't hand everything over without a fight.

"Don't know about any of that!" Tomsick answered him. "You must leave, or we will open fire!"

Chapter 23

Badgers

Before Tomsick had a chance to carry through with his threat, gunfire erupted from the other side of the compound. Some was automatic weapons fire, which would have been the soldiers. They were first and there weapons fire was followed by the volleys of single shot deer rifles, several volleys of deer rifles.

Steve didn't like the sound of it at all.

"What's it going to be, Ranger Brighton?"

"Surrender, Captain! What you are protecting is not worth it. We aren't bumpkins. We can assume you wanted dead sasquatch, to clone them. Your secret is out! Stand down, so no one gets hurt!"

No answer. Steve hoped that meant Tomsick was giving it some serious thought.

More gunfire could be heard from the other side. Steve got on the radio and called Milt.

"What in the hell is happening over there? Over."

"The General wanted a fight. We gave him one. Casualties on both sides. Mostly theirs. The General and a few of his men cut and ran. Over."

"Tomsick," Steve began, "my guys have taken the advantage on the other side of the compound. Your General has already pulled back. Just put down your weapons and save lives here!"

Steve saw movement behind the barricade.

The three doctors came to Tomsick.

"Captain, your General is unhinged," Doctor Nolte stated. "This is sheer madness to fight against armed citizens. We want out!"

Tomsick had to agree with the doctor's assessment. General Wartman had lost his direction and moral compass.

"Men, we're standing down! Lay down your weapons. We can't kill American citizens! Our job here is done!"

Tomsick dropped his own weapon and the ten men with him did the same.

"We're coming out, Ranger Brighton! Don't shoot!"

What happened next would be etched in Steve's memory until the day he died.

As Tomsick, his men, the three doctors and several lab assistants came out from behind the barricades, an alarm sounded. It sounded very similar to the type of alarm one would hear in movies when a submarine was preparing to do a dive.

Steve and his men had no clue what it meant, but it was loud. Steve felt a tightness in the pit of his stomach, because he knew it couldn't be good.

Tomsick and his group had cleared the barricade and were forty yards past it when the alarm went off. Even they looked confused.

Quick movements could be seen behind the barricades and loud chuffing sounds, like from a bull when exhaling as a warning to its enemy.

Doctor Nolte had time to yell, "BADGERS!" as seven huge beasts breached the barricade itself and headed straight for the unarmed group.

The things were ferocious, quick and deadly. The members of the group were running towards Steve and the hunters.

Steve yelled, "FIRE!" He hoped they could save some of the people in front of them.

The hunters began firing at the creatures. The problem was that they were moving around, clawing and gnashing at the unarmed group. To add insult to injury, the hunters didn't know where to shoot a ninety-pound badger to drop it. They had no knowledge for the positioning of a kill shot for these monsters.

Tomsick and his people were literally getting slaughtered. Pieces and parts were flying. Blood covered the ground. And the hunters kept pumping bullets into the creatures and unfortunately, into a few of those whom they were trying to save.

Badgers began to fall, but not quickly enough. Two badgers escaped into the woods. By the time the smoke had cleared, ten of the eleven soldiers, including Tomsick, were dead or dying. Doctors Nolte and Dougherty and two lab assistants also died in the scrum.

The only survivors were Doctor Ganse, three lab assistants and one soldier. The General had released the badgers and killed his own people.

The violent creatures were not drawn to those persons for any other reason than that they stood between the badgers and freedom. The badgers, being hyper aggressive due to the experiments performed on them and the drug cocktail that swam through their bloodstream, could not pass up an opportunity to maim, kill and destroy their foe.

The hunters were spared for now, but there was no telling how the two aggressive creatures that escaped would factor into future encounters. Steve was worried about them, but had a more pressing issue in front of him.

The General stood at the barricade. He was holding an M60 machine gun and a bandolier of bullets led from the weapon to a metal ammo box on the ground.

Steve and several hunters pulled the survivors to the ground as the General opened fire with the fearsome weapon.

Three hunters were not fortunate enough to make it to safety and were cut down. It didn't take but a few seconds for the hunters that were still under cover to chew up the General and drop him where he stood.

From behind the General, five soldiers emerged with their hands up. It was a Sergeant First Class, known as Cookie, and his men whom had fed the facility's occupants day and night.

Steve got Doctor Ganse to his feet, "How many more experiments like the badgers are there?"

"None," Ganse answered. "This second batch of sasquatch clones was to have priority. We killed all the other animals, except the badgers. They were the General's favorite."

"And the sasquatch clones? Where are they?" Steve asked.

"Follow me, Ranger Brighton," Ganse said, as he turned to lead the men to what had been called The Bigfoot Compound.

Once there, Steve couldn't believe what he was seeing. Three sasquatches were rolling around playing and socializing like children.

"I want to let my men see this for themselves and then, I guess we'll let them go," Steve suggested. He then quickly asked, "Or are they too dangerous or aggressive?"

"No, Ranger Brighton. They are not yet too aggressive or dangerous. But you can't let them go," Ganse informed him.

"Why?" Steve asked.

"There is a built-in fail/safe incorporated into their genetic code. We used a drug called ZZ-14. These clones cannot produce insulin in sufficient amounts to live. So we give them daily doses of insulin," Ganse explained.

"Why did you give them diabetes?" Steve inquired, very curious to hear the answer.

"In that way, if they escaped our control, like Clone C had done, they will quickly become ill and die. We couldn't let that happen again," the doctor further explained.

"What do you suggest we do with these three?" Steve continued with his questions.

"Terminate them. I no longer wish to be associated with such a project, and the other two are dead. So putting them down would be the most humane thing to do," the doctor explained. It made good sense to Steve and the others.

Steve allowed the hunters, who were able, to observe the sasquatches and know that such a beast exists in the wild. While some took advantage of the opportunity, others helped Steve and his rangers provide first aid and prepare to move the few wounded.

Because of the General's resistance, seven hunters died and four were wounded. Fifteen soldiers were killed, ten by the badgers and five who stood with the General. Three soldiers needed medical attention.

It turned out that Cookie was the ranking soldier. Steve put him in charge of his temporary prisoners. They totaled nineteen, once they were all gathered together.

Their zip ties were removed and they, with Cookie in charge, were asked to help transport the wounded. They were glad to do so.

When it came time to put down the juvenile sasquatch, Steve asked Doctor Ganse, "Can you just give them a shot? Shooting them seems unnecessarily cruel."

Ganse laughed, "Didn't you just march up here with all these men, ready to go to war? Men were killed, yet you feel a soft spot for these creatures?"

"Doctor, men usually make the decisions that get them killed. These creatures are not yet capable of making those choices. They are innocents living in a harsh world. Plus, as you pointed out, men died today. Let that be enough violence for a while."

"Brighton, I can respect that sentiment and to answer your original question, I can gently euthanize them. Let me get my medical bag."

The day was over. The battle won.

As they were making their way back to the busses, Steve remembered a Bible verse that was oddly haunting him.

Matthew 6:34 "Therefore do not worry about tomorrow, for tomorrow will worry about itself. Each day has enough trouble of its own."

Amen, he thought.

Chapter 24

Epilogue

The following day, Steve, Milt and the Toms were arrested by federal agents. They were taken to the abandoned facility that they had stormed the previous day.

The place was abuzz with military personnel, FBI and Homeland Security. The four men were locked up in a cell together. By the smell of it, it had recently been scrubbed and disinfected.

Steve assumed its previous occupants had been some sort of experimental animals. The place wasn't really meant to house prisoners.

A few hunters were paraded by their cell and presumably into their own cells. Steve wondered if they traced everyone back to the hunting club.

"Do you think we're in big trouble?" Milt asked.

"If there is any justice in this world, they are in trouble, not us. We haven't even been able to contact our lawyers. That's a civil rights violation."

"Damn, Steve! I don't even have a lawyer. Never needed one," Tom Deering admitted.

"Me neither," Tom Bollman said.

"Guys, if this goes ugly, I'll take the blame. You were just following my orders," Steve told them.

An agent, in sunglasses and a black suit with subtle pinstriping, stopped in front of their cell. He looked them over.

Tom Deering looked at the guy and said, "What are you going to do? Pull out your pen and erase our memories?"

"Very funny," the man said without cracking a smile. He then unlocked their cell and said, "Follow me."

They did as they were requested, more out of curiosity than obedience. They were taken down a hallway and then into a large conference room.

An older man in a suit was seated between two attractive, bookish looking women. Both had their hair up in a businesslike manner and wore glasses. The affectations could not hide their exceptional good looks.

"Have a seat, gentlemen. Please," the man held his hand out in an open gesture for them to feel welcome to be seated. They obliged.

He didn't waste any time, "So, what were you thinking attacking a secret military facility? What was it going to get you, did you imagine?"

The question was meant to unnerve them and put them on the defensive. Steve wasn't playing by his rules.

"It did and will get us justice. Your General was responsible for the deaths of several civilians who didn't deserve to die. And I don't care if your secrets here would cure cancer, end world hunger and bring peace to mankind. Those people didn't deserve to die!·

"And the monster that escaped from here killed even more people. So I suggest you let us talk to our lawyers, because you now are racking up civil rights violations as we speak."

"You must be Ranger Steve Brighton. I heard you're a force to be reckoned with. I now see that is true," the man complimented.

"You have us at a disadvantage. You seem to know who we are. Who the hell are you?" Steve asked. His men sat silently, more than willing to let Steve give the guy hell.

"My bad. I'm Senator Raymond Harberger. I'm the chairman of the Senate Committee on Homeland Security."

Steve kept up his attack, "Why would Homeland Security be in charge of a military facility that was experimenting on animals and preparing them to be monsters for war?"

Harberger wasn't about to be kept on the run by this man. He answered him truthfully.

"You see, Ranger Brighton, monsters can be used in all kinds of ways. If we could just get those badgers to follow commands, we could send them into drug runners' tunnels under the Mexico/American border. That would clear that problem right the hell up, wouldn't it?

"Or if protestors got out of hand, we could send in a company of sasquatches standing shoulder to shoulder. Who would mess with that? Monsters have all kinds of uses, here and overseas.

"So you see, Homeland gets to oversee these types of programs. But you shouldn't have attacked the facility. That is insurrection, punishable by some very stiff penalties," the man concluded.

"Do your worst, Senator. The amount of evidence I have collected will have you backpedaling for years. We'd like our lawyers now, please," Steve said testily. His patience was wearing thin.

"No need. If you will sign a non-disclosure agreement, we'll forget this ever happened. But you have to forget it too. General Wartman stepped way over the line. We regret that, truly. We can see where you felt you needed to do what you did, as good citizens."

Milt grabbed Steve's arm. "Take the deal, Steve. We want to get the hell out of here," he whispered.

"No repercussions. We keep our jobs. The IRS doesn't come after us. No campaign to assassinate us one by one. Life goes on. And this facility remains closed," Steve said by way of negotiation.

"Absolutely. But you must work on our behalf to keep the hunters from blowing everything out of proportion. We are talking a verbal and written blackout. Just let it die. This is what we are telling the hunters that we rounded up as well," the Senator explained.

"And if we can't contain it? If some of the hunters insist on running at the mouth?" Steve posed.

"As we are explaining to your rag tag army, the IRS is a mean bitch. And then a veiled threat of further punitive action. Do we understand one another, Ranger Brighton?"

"Me and the boys just want to get back to our day to day lives. Nothing more."

"Sign these papers with the ladies here, and we'll all be well with each other. Everything will be back to normal. No recriminations."

The rangers were dropped off back at their office.

Milt was the first to ask, "Do you believe it's going to be that easy, Steve?"

Steve sat at his desk and rubbed his jaw with his right hand.

"Well, boss?" Tom Deering asked. "Give it to us straight. What do you think happens next?"

"We'll have to see, guys. We'll have to see," was all Steve would say.

One week later, Ranger Milt Cox was killed in a deer hunting accident. He was struck down while out in the woods doing his job. He was helping a hunter whom had broken his leg from a fall out of a tree stand.

A stray bullet caught him in the throat. He died on the way to the hospital. No one knew where the bullet had come from.

Is this how the end begins? Steve wondered.

Made in the USA
Monee, IL
28 September 2024

8035b8f8-8133-40ff-9ce3-a7360b86480dR01